SCOUNDREL

THE PROTECTORS OF THE PACK BOOK FIVE

KEIRA BLACKWOOD

ALSO BY KEIRA BLACKWOOD

The Protectors of Sawtooth Peaks

Running to the Pack

Defending the Pack

Uniting the Pack

Howl for the Holidays

Revenge

The Protectors of Riverwood

Grizzly Bait

Grizzly Mate

Grizzly Fate

The Protectors of the Pack

Bodyguard

Enemies

Heir

Warrior

Scoundrel

The Protectors Unlimited

Can't Prove Shift

Suave as Shift

In Deep Shift

The Protectors Quick Bites

(with Eva Knight)

Midnight Wish

I Dream of Grizzly

The Ocean's Roar

To Catch a Werewolf

The Vampires of Scarlet Harbor

Pierced

Hunted

Ruled

Spellbound Shifters: Dragons Entwined

(with Liza Street)

Dragon Forgotten

Dragon Shattered

Dragon Unbroken

Dragon Reborn

Dragon Ever After

CHAPTER ONE

JETT

The icy cliff was a pillar of shelter in the wasteland of frozen tundra. Limestone walls jutted from it like gnarled claws. Besides the mountain, there was nothing to see for miles, only a white-gray haze and an unsettling gale that ensnared and pulled anyone who wandered toward the precipice like an insatiable demon hunting for its next meal.

Twirling blades faded from view as the chopper that had delivered me rose into the fog, but the whirring sound still lingered. The small landing pad was desolate, leaving me to find my own way.

Knowing this was only a visit didn't help the bile churning in the pit of my stomach. Too many times I'd envisioned myself ending up here. But I'd changed. The Ashwood chapter of the Silent Butchers had changed.

Unfortunately, our pasts hadn't changed. Going straight and taking jobs on the right side of the law didn't absolve us of our sins.

Tribunal Facility 17. Icicles hung from the silver lettering on the arch above the door. I'd never wanted to set foot in this place, but I didn't have a choice. I turned and looked out to the twenty-foot stone walls topped with razor-wire. Machine gun turrets were perched in watchtower spires and scanned the walkways below.

Tribunal Facility 17, The Meat Locker, was both a castle and a prison.

The doors opened before me, and a rush of warm air struck me in a surprising but welcome embrace. I glanced at the man holding the door for me—big, stoic, and clean-shaven. His uniform was pressed, suggesting a man of discipline, and his scent said bear. My guess—polar bear, given our location, though I wouldn't ask.

"Name?" The guard's eyes narrowed.

"Jett Greyson. I have an appointment to see my client, Keirnan Draper."

"ID?"

I pulled my identification from my briefcase, unsurprised that authentication was required. Again. I'd also supplied it before loading into the chopper that brought me here.

"You can't bring that in." The guard pointed to my briefcase.

"Sure." I handed it over. That wasn't a surprise, either, though I was supposed to record what Draper had to say, and my audio recorder was in my briefcase. "Can I take—"

"No pens, no pencils. No audio recording devices. You'll leave your cell phone, your wallet, your belt, your shoes—"

"My shoes? You want me to leave my shoes?"

"You'd be surprised what a desperate man could do with a shoelace."

Probably not. But I hesitated.

"Want this meeting to happen?" The guard lifted a brow.

Not really. I wanted to get the hell out of here. Still, I took off my shoes. "Yes."

He cracked a smile. "Lie."

"I'm a lawyer," I said. "It's my job."

He laughed, a dry, dark sound. "All right, lawyer, spread 'em."

I leaned my palms against the cold stone wall and did as I was told. Thankfully, his callused hands patted and invaded no longer than was necessary. He took my shoes, my wallet, and my phone, then slapped his badge over a panel on the wall.

A stone door opened slowly, followed by a second door made of metal. Another guard waited on the other side, dressed just like the first, with the same stoic look and dead eyes.

I stepped through the threshold and listened to the doors slam shut behind me. The sound resonated through my chest and echoed down the empty gray hall. My focus needed to be on the meeting ahead, but it was hard to tune out the panicked feeling of being trapped inside the most feared shifter prison in existence.

The guard led me down the hall to an elevator, where he used a card to activate the controls.

"Step in."

I did, and the doors slid shut, leaving me alone as I sank deep into the heart of the prison. The numbers above the door went up, though I was most definitely going down. I rolled my shoulders, stretching the stiff fabric of my jacket. The sooner this was over, the sooner I could lose the suit and throw on a pair of jeans. Give me leather and denim over Armani any day.

The elevator stopped at 15, and the doors opened once more. Fifteen stories down into the side of the mountain. Was this where the roving chapter was being held? That, or it was just the location used for meetings. Given my experience so far, and the horror stories I'd heard about this place, it didn't seem likely that there were many visitors.

I stepped out into an open room. Everything was painted gray. The air was damp and frigid, and filled with the wild scent of shifters. No, not just any shifters—wolves.

The number 15 was painted by the elevator, and again on the other side of the room. There were five doors, all exactly the same, and I had no idea which one I was supposed to open.

"Hello?" My voice bounced around the room with no reply.

A door opened, the one on the right.

Inside the room was dark, and the lights only flicked on as I stepped in. The door shut behind me, and my inner wolf howled and clawed to be released, hating the idea of being detained. I could only imagine how the prisoners felt.

In the center of the room was a box of glass, and standing by the edge was a man. His hair was shaved off, his beard, too. But his eyes—those I recognized—icy gray, and twice as hard. I knew little about the man, only that he was VP of the Silent Butchers roving chapter, second to the alpha. We'd met only once, a couple of years back.

The rovers had never put down roots in any particular city like the rest of us had, and instead wandered the country following wherever money led them. As the closest chapter to where the rovers were arrested, the burden fell to the Ashwood chapter to investigate what went wrong. I was here for Draper's story.

"Hawke sent his number two instead of coming himself?" Draper's voice cracked as if it was the first time he'd spoken in a while, and he squinted up at the lights.

"You know that's not how this works." Hawke, my alpha, would never set foot in this place—that was one of the perks of being alpha, I guessed. I approached the glass, taking note of the chair that was welded to the floor next to it.

"By all means," Draper said, "have a seat."

Hard pass. "Tell me what happened."

"What, no pleasantries? You know how long it's been since I had contact with the outside world? How long it's been since anyone even fucking looked at me?"

"Too long, I'm sure." Fourteen months since apprehension, since rumors of an ambush had started. I'd thought we'd never be granted a meeting.

"If Hawke wasn't coming himself, he should've sent a piece of ass. What I wouldn't give to see a nice set of tits. You have nice tits, Greyson?"

I clenched my jaw. We only had thirty minutes. That could have started when I arrived or when I stepped off the elevator, I had no way to know. Whichever way it went, Draper was wasting what little time we had left.

"Tell me what happened in Greenville or I walk." It was said that the rovers were picked up outside of Greenville City, and that Dirty Jack, Draper's alpha, was dead. If I was lucky whatever landed the rovers in a cell was their own fault, and it wasn't my problem. Hawke seemed to think that was the case, but we weren't in Greenville City when it happened, and we had to know for sure.

"We were betrayed, plain and simple." Draper shrugged and turned around, feigning disinterest.

"Who betrayed you?"

"Same guy who hired us—Briggs."

That didn't make any sense. Why the hell would the Greenville City Pack hire the Butchers, only to betray them? "What was the job?"

Draper looked up to the ceiling, to the little speaker in the corner. They were listening. Of course they were listening.

"Briggs told us to meet him in the forest. We did as we were told, and that's where we got ambushed. Briggs's brother told us where to find the asshole after that, but when we got there, all we found was *Tribunal scum.*" The vein in his neck pulsed and he clenched his fists as he yelled at the ceiling.

The rovers were twice fucked over by the same family. "What about Dirty Jack? There were rumors—"

"Briggs killed him."

I studied Draper's rage-contorted face. Everything he said was true. I'd have heard it if he was lying.

The situation was worse than Hawke had thought.

The door opened, and a guard stepped inside. This was a different guy than the two I'd seen upstairs. "Time to go."

"Wait!" Draper banged his fists on the glass. "Wait!"

I turned back.

"Sure you don't want to show me those tits? Come on, Greyson. I know they're nice."

The guard pushed a series of buttons on the screen on his forearm. Sprinklers in the glass cube turned on and soaked Draper. Water ran down his face, and the crazed sound of his laughter haunted me long after I walked away.

* * *

THE WAY back was just one motion after another, given it was a two-day trip. I reclaimed my belongings and was flown back to the little town of Frozen Peaks. From there, I took my motorcycle. I considered calling Hawke to report, but he'd want to hear this in person.

At first the roads were icy patches of black, indistinguishable from the pavement. I wasn't in the best state to deal with that kind of shit, and my tires slipped more than once on the curved mountain roads. The frigid air bit my skin right through my clothes, and again I wished I'd been wearing my usual jeans and leather instead of this monkey suit.

The farther I drove, the more the scenery transformed. Bare-branched oaks replaced snow-coated pines. The scents of the air grew richer, revealing layers of life and decay. This was what summer forests were meant to be, none of that flat dampness of frost. Soon, I'd be home.

Draper's words haunted me as the wind whipped and the birds chirped. We weren't just dealing with a fuckup by the roving chapter, getting caught by the Tribunal. We were dealing with a declaration of war from the Greenville City Pack.

Sure, Draper was losing his shit, but who wouldn't when trapped in a dark cell in isolation? He was off, but from what I could tell, not delusional. And he hadn't lied. Not once.

I knew Hawke well enough to be sure he wouldn't let the Greenville City Pack's betrayal slide. No matter how hard the Ashwood Silent Butchers were working to make a living respectably—trading questionable mercenary jobs for respectable security gigs—we still had an obligation to our brothers. Fuck with the Butchers, face the consequences.

Hawke would want to hear everything from me firsthand the moment I returned to Ashwood, and I knew better than to keep him waiting. The engine beneath me purred as I crested the last hilltop and cruised down into the little valley town that was home. The pavement was rough and jostled my tires, a familiar feeling on the old streets. I'd spent my life in this town, leaving only for law school, then returning to my roots, here in Ashwood. My father was a Butcher, and his father before him. The MC and the pack, they were one in this town, and they were my family.

As I parked behind the two-story brick building that was both our place of business and our clubhouse, I could feel the weight of someone watching. No surprise there, since Hawke was waiting.

The door burst open. I climbed from my bike and turned.

It wasn't Hawke who stood waiting, but Brick. The six and a half-foot grizzly shifter always stomped when he walked, but this time he was hunched in a strange way, with his arm behind him.

His hard, brown eyes set on me. All the color drained from his face, and he looked like he'd been through hell.

"What the fuck happened, Brick?"

I steeled myself for whatever had done this to him, to beat the hell out of whoever deserved it.

He opened his mouth and shut it again.

"Shit going down inside?" I asked. "I'll go in and—"

"No." He pulled out the thing that was behind him, the thing that had him keeled over like he was injured. He shoved it forward, and stood up straight. "This is it."

Before me stood a little kid, a blond-haired girl with bright blue eyes and the kind of scowl that said she was trouble. Trouble that hated Brick.

"I'm not a *this*," she said. "*I'm a person.*"

"She's yours." Brick nodded at me.

"What the hell is that supposed to mean?"

Brick backpedaled toward the door. "I hate to be the one to tell you...but apparently you have a daughter. Welcome home, Greyson."

Brick ducked inside, and the door shut behind him. The kid crossed her arms and frowned at me.

What the fuck? This had to be some kind of misunderstanding...or a shitty prank...or... Fuck.

CHAPTER TWO

PAIGE

*S*taring at an empty Word file, I tapped my fingers softly over the keys. My butt was parked in my favorite writing chair, in the comfort of my living room. It was usually the best place in the world to work. Coffee cup number three was kicking in, filling me with caffeiney goodness. The twitchy energy was there, but the words...not so much.

When I'd taken a job at *Gimme,* the love and lifestyle blog, I'd thought I was just one chance away from meeting Mr. Right. I'd thought life always ended up like the movies, where the perfect guy would show up at the most awkward time and it would be kismet. Then I'd have my story, the perfect article where I'd know exactly what to say about relationships. He'd see me in a way I'd never seen myself, not as the awkward chubby girl, but as a goddess of pure perfection.

I figured it'd be easy. Shifters were supposed to have one true mate fated to complete us, two halves of a whole. Back home, I knew from a young age who my mate wasn't. He wasn't anyone I'd met. Bear men were cocky lumberjacks, and *not* for me.

As soon as I could escape, I ran off to college and surrounded myself with humans. They didn't expect me to be a certain way because of my heritage. But that wasn't working out so well, either.

Five years I'd been writing for *Gimme*, and I was tired of looking for Mr. Right in a stream of not so great Mr. Right Nows. Hope and optimism faded to weariness from expecting some amazing lust and devotion-filled inspiration to crash into my life.

So even though I wanted to write the perfect article about mind-blowing sex and intense spiritual connection, or hell, even a glimpse at something close to either, I settled. I compromised, like I always did, by flipping through the early editions of next month's fashion magazines for some new trend I didn't hate.

Tiny backpacks, crocheted crop tops, short skinny wide-legged jeans...how did that even...never mind. There, on page twelve, was something I could pretend to be passionate about—high-waisted, loose cotton pants. My go-to was yoga pants, for sure, but when it was time to stop writing and put on my real pants, I was one hundred percent behind something that looked comfy while also being chic.

Settled on the subject of my next article—a ballad of love and devotion...to comfortable pants—I traded my yoga pants for a black linen pair of palazzos with billowy legs and a high waist from my closet. A quick mirror selfie of the pants in question, and I was ready to write.

Screw stiff jeans. Gimme comfort. Gimme a pair of palazzos paired with a crop top and wedges.

No, wedges were out, no matter how comfortable they were. And I wouldn't actually be caught dead baring my midsection, but that was beside the point. The fashion crowd liked crazy high heels and hearing how great short shirts were. Hmm...

Glitz and sparkle are nice enough. But a girl's best friend has nothing to do with diamonds, it's comfortable pants.

It was relatable, but it wasn't *Gimme* material. Ugh. I clicked the laptop shut. At some point I'd have to finish this article or I wouldn't make rent. But "at some point" wasn't right now, so yay for that.

Visiting Evie was something I'd both been looking forward to and dreading for the last week. I grabbed my keys and the plush unicorn from the top of my dresser and headed out the door.

Her mother Marla and I had been inseparable since kindergarten, gluing our hands together as an excuse to keep our playdates going. It never worked, but we kept trying. As we got older, it was softball. She'd always been the athletic one, and I played just to hang out with her. And when she got knocked up by some asshat, I was there to share in the joy when her baby was born.

That's what made my visit today hard. Marla died in a car accident three years ago, and she didn't get to watch Evie grow up. I was determined to visit every couple of months and show my best friend's daughter that I still cared, even when it was hard. She looked just like Marla, except for her eyes, and she certainly had her mother's sass. Being together was a bittersweet reminder of what I'd lost.

Evie lived with her grandmother Linda just over an hour away. With the plush unicorn on the seat next to me, I left my apartment in the middle of the city and headed to the suburbs. The throng of taxis slowly subsided, while the buildings grew shorter and farther apart.

As I drove, my mind wandered. How big would Evie be this time? It seemed like she shot up a few inches every time I visited. She was already seven. I bet by the time she was ten or eleven she'd be as tall as me. Would she even like unicorns anymore? It wasn't just kids' sizes that seemed to change constantly, but their interests, too.

The drive wasn't terribly long, and before I knew it, I was there. Up ahead, the Flint house had an unfamiliar car in the driveway. I pulled up to the curb, parked, and grabbed the unicorn when I climbed out.

On my way up the sidewalk, I fidgeted with the unicorn's horn. I was even more of a ball of nerves this time than last time. It was silly. Everything was fine. Evie would be happy to see me, and I'd get to hear about her life, and then I'd go home and the painful memory of losing my best friend would fade once again. Worrying only made it worse.

I womaned up and knocked. A few moments later, the door opened, and a somewhat familiar face greeted me in the doorway.

"Sylvia?" I said. I hadn't seen Marla's aunt in ten years at least. Her face was wrinkled in a perpetual frown, one that she was reinforcing as she looked me over.

"Who are you?" she asked.

"I'm Paige, Marla's friend. Is Linda home?"

Sylvia's shoulders sank as she squeezed the door handle. "No."

I considered asking what was wrong, but she seemed more likely to bite my head off than open up. "Do you know when she'll be back? She's expecting me."

"A few months, if she's lucky."

"What?"

"Linda broke her hip. She'll be in a rehabilitation center for weeks if not months. She's not going to be here for your…" She looked down at the unicorn clutched in my arms. "Whatever you're doing together."

Seriously, what was with the attitude? I didn't remember her being friendly, but this was uncalled-for bitchiness.

"What about Evelyn?" I asked. "Where is she?"

It was summer break. She shouldn't have been at school, and she couldn't have followed her grandmother into rehab.

"Linda can't take care of that little hellion. Barely could before, and she certainly can't now."

"Where. Is. She?"

"Where she belongs. With her *daddy.*" Sylvia shook her head and squared her shoulders.

I just stared at her, shocked. Evie had her grandmother, and she had me. That was it, the whole damned circle of support.

In a prim voice, she said, "I dropped her off yesterday."

"How could you?" I couldn't believe it. My chest ached for the poor child. "Jett Greyson doesn't even know her. He's a shitty—"

"Language, missy." Sylvia narrowed her eyes and tilted her chin up.

Yeah, no.

"Fuck manners," I said. "Tell me where the hell you took her, and tell me now. That little girl doesn't belong in a place like that. Do you have any idea—" I sucked in a deep breath.

Sylvia's disapproval seemed to soften just a hint when she looked into my eyes. "I'll give you the address, but remember she's his daughter."

"Yeah, thanks." I tried to keep the bitterness out of my tone. I was grateful for the address, even if I was pissed as hell that Sylvia had just given Evie away like she didn't matter. Well, she mattered to me, even when it was hard. *Especially* when it was hard.

Jett Greyson was a womanizing asshat. I'd heard all about him from Marla, about how he'd made her believe he loved her, then never called her again after they'd fucked. He was a biker, a criminal, and a scumbag. The last place Evelyn should be was with Jett Greyson.

CHAPTER THREE

JETT

*H*er skinny little legs dangled from the bar stool like twigs waving in the wind, the only indication of the child's discomfort. A stoic little statue, except for her feet, the girl stared up at me with the same cold slate eyes that greeted me in the mirror. Was it a coincidence, or was I really this girl's father?

I reached over the bar and filled two glasses—one with beer, one with water. I knew next to nothing about children, but at least I knew not to feed them alcohol. "What's your name, squirt?"

"Evelyn."

"Evelyn what?"

"Flint."

I scoured my memory for a chick with that last name, but I came up short. How long were we talking anyway? Five years? Ten?

"How old are you?"

"How old are *you?*" Evelyn scowled.

All right, so she was a tough little twerp. I appreciated that. "What's your mom's name?"

She crossed her arms and leaned back against the counter. "I don't have a mom."

"You just spawned out of a pit somewhere?"

"Maybe."

"Okay, Evelyn Flint, Fearsome Pit Spawn, tell me, why are you here?"

"Because..." Her lip quivered, a shake in that hard resolve.

My chest tightened, and I straightened my back.

Shit. This wasn't the kind of interrogation I was used to. I'd have to be...softer. I'd have to tread carefully and watch what I said. What the hell would I do if she started to cry?

Her blue eyes glossed and she looked down.

What the fuck was I supposed to say?

The door opened behind me. "Greyson."

I turned and found Hawke standing in the threshold.

He said, "Come with me."

A short reprieve, but I knew this conversation wasn't going to be any easier than the one with the kid.

I rose from my seat, and looked down at Evelyn. "Don't move."

She met my gaze and said nothing. I took the eye contact to mean my order was understood, and then I followed Hawke down the hall.

"What's with the kid?" He kept his gaze forward and his shoulders squared.

"Not sure yet, but I'll handle it."

With a curt nod, Hawke opened the door to his office. I followed him in and shut the door behind us.

He faced me from the other side of his desk. "Tell me about the Meat Locker."

I knew exactly what he wanted to hear—reassurance that Dirty Jack, alpha of the roving Butchers, had fucked up in Greenville. He wanted me to say that it wasn't our problem. I wished I could tell him that.

"Draper says Briggs hired him, then turned on them. They sicced the Tribunal on the rovers and killed Dirty Jack."

Hawke's fists twisted on the top of the chair. "Why the fuck would Greenville do this?"

By the way he looked down at the table, it didn't seem like he expected an answer. Still, I had to say something. "I don't know."

"No chance he's lying?" Hawke searched my face, but his intense, hazel eyes told me he already knew the answer.

"No."

Hawke bashed his hands on the top of his seat and threw it. The chair screeched across the hardwood and slammed into the wall. Better the chair than me.

Hawke's chest heaved and his face was red. "What the fuck am I supposed to do, Jett? You know as well as I do that going after Greenville will fuck up everything we're building here."

"I know." It hadn't been easy, but we'd built a reputable security business. After the Tribunal had intervened on the Juarez job, Hawke had decided it was time. We'd backslid when the only clients we could find to put food on the table wanted merc jobs. But after lean months and a hell of a time, we'd built a thriving security business. It was all due to Hawke's leadership. None of the other chapters had managed to do the same, though a few had tried. But all of that went to shit if we made a mistake now. The Tribunal could be watching, and even if they weren't, I respected what Hawke had built for us.

"You know what Brick's going to say?" Hawke shot me a look.

"Retribution." No question there.

He nodded. "I can't let this slide."

"I know." I wished he could—hell, I knew he did, too.

He stared at the table, searching for answers in the grain of the wood.

Hawke had two advisors, me and Brick. Everyone else was away visiting the Glendon Chapter. I had to offer something. If it was up to Brick, there'd be lives lost. Brick always had a plan.

But maybe I could prevent bloodshed. I had to offer an alternative. "I'll go."

Hawke met my gaze and ran a hand through his blond hair.

"Let me scout them, see what I can learn. If we can determine Briggs's motivation, there might be a way out." *Please, let there be a way out.*

Hawke's shoulders eased. "Do it."

I nodded. Good. But there was an issue to resolve first—the kid. "There's something personal I have to deal with first. I'll head to Greenville City in the morning."

"All right." Hawke clasped my shoulder as I turned for the door. "Jett, find me a peaceful solution."

"I will." Without question, it would be a challenge, one I meant to rise to and conquer. I'd drive to Greenville and see what there was to find...after I figured out what the hell I was going to do with the kid. First thing had to be learning if she really was mine.

Back by the bar, the stools were empty. Maybe the kid had to go to the bathroom. There was someone behind the bar. Thick black hair and bare shoulders, Shaundra was messing with the glasses.

"Hey," I said, "did you see where the kid went?"

Shaundra turned, a glass and drying rag in her hands. "You mean Ray?"

"No, not the prospect, a real kid. Little girl. I left her sitting on this stool."

Shaundra furrowed her brow and looked up at me. "This is no place for a child."

I slammed my fist down on the bar. "Did you see her or not?"

"Nope. Just got in. Haven't seen anyone yet, except for your grumpy ass."

I checked the bathroom, and it was empty, then I rushed outside.

As the door clicked shut behind me, I heard Shaunda's voice. "You're welcome."

I scanned the lot, but the kid wasn't there. There was a pang in my chest, a tightness. Where'd she go?

I cupped my hands and called out, "Evelyn."

Guilt and concern weighed on me. Sure, I didn't want to have to deal with a kid, but that didn't mean I wanted something bad to happen to her. Please, don't let something bad have happened to her.

There was a scraping sound. I turned the corner of the building, and there stood Evelyn by the flower bed, kicking a piece of mulch across the pavement. A weight lifted from my chest. Now that I wasn't worried, I was pissed.

"I told you to stay."

Her lips flattened into a line. "That's what people say to dogs."

I guessed it was. "I didn't mean it like that."

She shrugged her shoulders and stared down at the mulch, crushing the wood chunk beneath her heel.

I tried to remember what it was like to be her age, not that I knew how old she was. Most of what I remembered was my parents fighting, and me running off to play with Hawke out in the forest. We'd built a tree fort with his old man while I avoided my fucked-up home life. It wasn't a helpful memory.

"What do kids like?" I asked.

Evelyn looked up at me and I stilled in her gaze. She looked so young, so lost. And it made me feel shitty, and I was a bit surprised that it did. It was strange the effect she had on me. I cared that she wasn't happy, that someone had abandoned her, leaving her in the care of a total stranger. I felt bad for her, and I didn't want to make her feel worse.

"What do kids like to do nowadays?" I repeated myself.

"You sound like an old man."

"Not that old," I said. Though she was right. I did.

"Why do you care?" she asked. "I thought you didn't like me."

"I don't know you," I said. "You don't know me. You tell me something you like, and I'll do the same."

"You go first."

"Hmmm." Sex. Shifting. Those weren't appropriate. She carried the wild scent of a shifter, but if her mother was human, she likely didn't know anything about what that meant. Pointing to my motorcycle I said, "Riding my bike."

"You like bikes?" Her brows lifted and her shoulders relaxed.

It was beginning to look like we'd found common ground. "Hell yeah. Want to see?"

"Okay."

She walked up next to me, but kept her distance. I led her around to where my pride and joy was parked. "Here she is."

"Did you say *she*?" Evelyn's eyes narrowed and a smiled played on the corner of her lips.

"Hell yeah I said she. Motorcycles are meant to be treated with respect. And every good bike has a name—a *girl's* name." I was just making shit up, but the kid was engaging.

She reached a tentative hand out and touched the leather seat. "What's hers?"

"Evelyn."

"No way."

I shrugged. "Doesn't matter if you believe me. It's true."

She stared at the bike, which had never had a name until now, and then she looked back up at me. "Ice cream."

"Is that your bike's name? Some little red tricycle named Ice Cream?"

"Are you teasing me?" Evelyn narrowed her eyes and put her hands on her hips. "I *mean,* I like ice cream. You asked what kids like. *I* like ice cream."

"Ice cream, okay." There was a place on Wellington, just two blocks down from the clinic. Perfect.

"With hot fudge. And sprinkles."

"Sprinkles are shit."

Her eyes went wide. What did I do? I thought we had some decent banter going.

I cleared my throat. "One stop, and then I'll take you to get some ice cream."

"One stop?"

"Yeah."

"Deal." A victorious smile overtook her face.

It wasn't really supposed to be a bargain, but if she was happy, I was happy to leave it be.

I straddled my bike and offered her a hand. "Climb on."

She took it, and struggled to find footing.

Brick stepped out of the clubhouse and jogged toward us. His always hard face was a little harder than usual. Maybe Hawke had told him about my trip to the Meat Locker. "What the hell, Greyson?"

"I have shit to do," I said. "We can talk about Draper later."

"What? No. I'm talking about this." He waved his arms at me and Evelyn. "You can't take a kid that small on a bike."

"Why not?"

"There's safety laws and shit. Don't you know anything about kids?"

"No. Not really."

"Here." He fished his keys from his pocket and held them out. "Take my truck."

Well, I didn't want to hurt the kid, and I really was entirely lost, so I accepted and climbed off. Probably not a bad idea, since she still hadn't gotten herself on the back.

"Thanks." I gave Brick a salute and looked to Evelyn. She was staring down at the ground, her shoulders hanging. She looked like a deflated version of the spitfire she could be. Were all kids this expressive, or just her? Either way, it was nice to be able to read her.

"There'll still be hot fudge," I said.

"And sprinkles."

"Okay, and sprinkles."

We walked side by side over to the truck, and I opened the door for her. But before either of us could climb in, Shaundra ran out and insisted we needed a plastic block for the kid to sit on top of, and kindly lended us one.

Evelyn put her hands up on the floor, reaching for something to grip, then she threw her leg up, trying to get a knee in. It was even more awkward for her trying to climb up into the lifted truck than it had been to get on the bike.

"Want some help?"

"I'm good."

She hooked her knee, and found her grip on the bottom of the seat. Her little arms and legs strained, and I respected how scrappy she was.

I said, "Looks like you could use a little help."

"I...can..."

I grabbed the foot that was still on the ground and lifted her. She was so light, hardly weighing anything at all. Brick was right, she would have blown away in the wind on the back of my bike.

She scrambled in, pulling her foot away as fast as she could.

I shut the door and climbed in the driver's seat.

"When you said bike, I thought you meant the kind with pedals and stuff."

"Oh yeah?" I turned the key and the engine roared.

She looked out her window. "I really wanted to go for a ride."

"When you're big enough not to fall off, we'll give it a go."

I could feel her gaze assessing me as I pulled from the lot and started to drive.

"You shouldn't make promises."

I glanced over at her, but she was already looking back out her window. I could appreciate how she felt, not that I'd ever been promised much, but the few that were made when I was her age, well, they were all broken. And it hurt like hell.

"Okay, no promises," I said. Honestly, I shouldn't have suggested anything beyond the ice cream. I was supposed to be wrapping this shit up. Go get a blood test, find out the kid isn't mine, figure out where I could return her. But I kind of liked her, and I didn't want to be another source of disappointment. Life was hard enough without me making it worse.

* * *

THERE WAS a painting of a cat man on the wall across from me in the doctor's waiting room. It had blue fur and a pile of dishes and household items piled up in its hands as it balanced with one foot on a beach ball. I couldn't figure out if it was supposed to be funny or creepy. I considered asking the kid sitting in front of it, but he was busy trying to bury his second knuckle up his nose while his mother ignored him for the screen in her palm.

I wasn't sure how long I'd been waiting, but even if the clinic took ten times longer than another office, I'd pick this place every time. Dr. Webber was a shifter, a valued member of the pack, and the only one I'd trust with this task. No question, Evelyn was in good hands.

Still, I was jittery. What if the results said that she was my daughter? What if it came back that she wasn't? It was easier if I could drop her off somewhere, be done. I told myself that was what I wanted, but what if it wasn't?

The image of Evelyn's trembling lip filled my head, along with the big doe eyes she'd given me as the nurse had taken her back the hall. *You're not going to leave me, right?* Her voice had been so soft, so small. I promised I wouldn't leave. Of course I wouldn't leave.

"Mr. Greyson." I looked up and found the nurse waiting for me in the doorway.

I followed her back the hall to one of the exam rooms. Evelyn was sitting on the table, white as a ghost.

Her expression was soft, and vulnerable. I wasn't sure if I should offer to hold her hand or if I should sit in the chair and give her some distance. I settled on standing near the table, but still giving her space.

"Mr. Greyson." Dr. Webber stood beside her and placed a hand on Evelyn's shoulder. She didn't acknowledge him, only looked at me. "Congratulations. You're a father."

A father.

Evelyn was my daughter.

The doctor was still talking, but I didn't hear what he was saying. Instead, all I could hear was the fluttering heartbeat of the child in front of me. All I could see were her wide eyes, the same blue as mine, the way she crinkled the table's paper covering between her fingers.

She was as terrified as I was.

But I felt something else after hearing those words—relief. I wanted her to be mine. Sure, it would take time to figure out how not to be a shitty parent. I'd had terrible parents of my own, but selfishly, it was nice to realize I wouldn't spend my life alone anymore.

CHAPTER FOUR

PAIGE

$\mathcal{U}$nicorn strapped in the passenger seat, booster seat from Linda's place and an overnight bag for me in the back, I was hightailing it to Ashwood. It wasn't like I had anything tying me to my place, so if this took more than one day, so be it. I could work anywhere, and the only one relying on me was the stray cat that showed up at my window sill on occasion. I'd named him Graybeard for his pirate-like missing eye and for the floof under his chin. But I'd left a note for my neighbor to leave him a can of tuna. Plus, for all I knew, Graybeard had another name and another family. Or three. He wasn't exactly thin, which made him all the more endearing.

The flutter in my chest wasn't from excitement. It wasn't the too-much-coffee kind either. Okay, maybe it was a little from the coffee, but mostly it was nerves.

I'd never actually met Jett Greyson. I had heard a hell of a lot about him, though, and the memory left me with a sour taste in the back of my throat.

Back in college, Jett walked into the coffeehouse where Marla was working at the time. It was a regular thing, coffee each Friday morning. She'd come back to our dorm, flop on the bed, and shower me in details of the way the light glittered off his eyes or the way he smiled when he left her way too big of a tip. She told me how he'd brush her finger when he took his cup, and how a gentle flirtation turned into something more. It was the perfect start to a beautiful love story, or so it seemed.

One date was all it took for her to fall in love with him, if she wasn't already. One night of passionate sex, and she was ready to do anything for him.

But then he stopped coming into the coffee shop. He didn't return her calls.

And she found out she was pregnant.

When she finally tracked him down, he wasn't at the law school he said he was attending, but in some shitty little town in the middle of nowhere. The bastard wasn't even a lawyer. He was a biker, and when she found him, he was in bed with two other women.

He said he didn't want anything to do with her or the baby. He said Evie wasn't his.

Fucking prick.

Now it was my turn to drive to that same shitty little town to confront Jett Greyson. For all I knew, he'd left Evie alone on his doorstep to fend for herself.

Tightening my grip on the steering wheel, I dropped my foot down harder on the accelerator. I needed to find Evie. Now.

"Hold on tight, Mr. Unicorn." I glanced down at the stuffed animal beside me, decided yes, I had consumed too much caffeine, and turned on the radio to sing my way out of some of this nervous energy. Before I knew it, I'd found the little town I was looking for.

I wasn't entirely sure what I'd been expecting—something somewhere between a junkyard of barbed wire-topped hovels and a trailer park perched in the bowels of hell.

Ashwood didn't look like either, at least not on the surface.

As I drove past lush spring gardens and quaint cottages, I reminded myself that appearances could be deceiving. When Marla had talked about how terrible this place was, her focus was likely on the people, and also seen through the lens of betrayal.

I didn't know what the clubhouse would look like, or even if Jett would be there. What if Sylvia had dropped Evie somewhere Jett didn't even live anymore? Why didn't I think to ask more questions before I left?

No. This wasn't helping. I needed to stop thinking and focus on looking. The clubhouse would be around here somewhere, and Evie would be fine. I'd take her home, not that I knew what would happen after that. She could stay with me until her grandmother was back on her feet. Yep. That was a solution. That was *the* solution.

I wouldn't need my laptop or the extra clothes I'd packed, since I'd just be grabbing Evie and heading back. But it always paid to be prepared. I'd learned that young, to always keep extra clothes around no matter where I was headed, because sometimes a girl had to shift. And it was really unfortunate if there was nothing to wear when a yellow sundress ended up in ribbons.

Something caught my eye, and I turned before I realized what exactly it was.

Standing in a small lot on the side road was the back of a little girl with long golden hair, just like Marla's. She had on a red dress, and she was just about the right height and build to be Evelyn.

I hit the brakes and wrenched the wheel to the right, parking abruptly by the curb.

I grabbed the stuffed unicorn from the passenger seat and ran around to the front of the building. There she was, sitting on a bench, completely alone.

"Evie!" I ran across the grass and fell to my knees, pulling the sweet, not-as-little-as-I-remembered girl into my arms.

She gave me a pat on the back, and pulled away.

"Hey, hon, how are you doing?" I smiled at her.

"Paige?" She furrowed her brow. "What are you doing here?"

"I'm here to take you home. Come on." I took her hand in mine and pulled gently.

"Wait," she said.

"Do you have a bag? Did Aunt Sylvia leave it somewhere?"

"Yes, but—"

"Don't worry." I turned back and kept walking, smiling down at her. "You're not alone anymore. I'm going to take you—"

I smashed into something hard. Something solid and unyielding, that smelled warm like spiced cider by the fire on a cold winter day, wild like the forest, like a shifter. Something that sent a jolt of electricity straight to my core. Something *wow*.

A thick arm reached around me, and caught me before I could fall back. A strong, muscular, tan arm, with intricate lines of black ink swirling up the massive bicep. I wanted to follow those lines, trace them with my finger up under the sleeve of his t-shirt just to see where they went. And see what other delicious surprises I might find.

Wait, what?

I squeezed Evelyn's hand and tried to move around the sexy bicep. But the guy attached to it stepped with me.

"Sorry about that," I said. "Excuse me."

I looked up and the apologetic smile on my face melted into what I can only assume was a drooling gape.

He was tall with broad shoulders, a chiseled jaw that had the perfect amount of hair to tickle and scratch in the best way, and big arms built for lifting. He had the hard masculinity that showed he didn't take shit from anyone. His eyes were blue as the sky, and sharp as they seemed to appraise me. I had no idea what he was thinking, but I was pretty sure I needed to rein in my crazy or I was bound to lick him.

"I, uh...was just." Yeah, it wasn't working.

"You're going to have to let go of my daughter." His voice was deep and rough, and it fit him. I found myself staring, not quite comprehending the words he'd said.

"What?"

"Did you get me double sprinkles?" I turned and found Evie looking up at Mr. Sexy Ink with a glint of excitement in her eyes. She pulled her hand from mine.

"I did," he said, still keeping his eyes glued to me. God, I melted under that cerulean gaze.

Finally, he broke the spell and leaned over, handing Evie a cone of vanilla ice cream topped in fudge and sprinkles. I enjoyed watching the way his arm and shoulder moved, the flex of his muscles, the...*holy fuck.*

"You're not Jett Greyson." I knew that sounded stupid. It sounded stupid to me and I'd been the one to produce the words.

"I am." Mr. Sexy Ink—Jett—stood up, holding a second cone in his hand. "Do you know Evelyn, Ms.—"

Here I was thinking I was rescuing the kid, and he was taking her out for ice cream.

"This is Paige," Evie told Jett, because apparently I'd lost the ability to speak for myself.

"Care to join us for ice cream?" he asked.

I cleared my throat and steeled my resolve. "I'm here for Evie. Nothing more."

That's right, don't fall for his charm. You know better, dammit!

"How do you two know each other?" Jett's gorgeous blue eyes scanned my face and I felt my cheeks heat. A droplet of melted ice cream dripped down over his big hand. I watched the drop of sweet cream move across his skin, and that urge to lick...well yeah.

An intense darkness flashed through his eyes like he could read my mind. Then he lifted the cone and dragged his tongue over his finger and up the side of the ice cream. A shot of desire flooded through me, as if it was my skin beneath his tongue.

"How do we know each other?" I repeated his question like an idiot, and the answer reminded me what I was supposed to be saying. I was supposed to be pissed, pissed as hell. "I'm Marla's best friend."

"Who's Marla?" There was genuine confusion in the look he gave me.

What the fuck? How many broken hearts had this guy left in his wake? How many women had he knocked up and discarded?

"You've got a lot of nerve, assho—jerk." I changed my words remembering that this whole thing was going down in front of a kid, but my sentiment remained the same. "You are the absolute worst."

He blinked hard, but that was the only reaction I got out of him. And that pissed me off even more.

"I don't know who you think you're going to fool with this ice cream stunt, but I'm not falling for it. I'm taking Evie, and we're going home."

"No." Jett took Evie's hand, and she willingly moved beside him.

"No?"

"You're not taking her." His voice was a growl, low and threatening as he stepped between me and Evelyn. There it was, the true Jett Greyson, the cold-hearted killer I'd heard so much about.

That crazy jittery feeling I'd had on the way here, well, it kicked up tenfold. I leaned in closer to him, unwilling to be intimidated. "Why are you doing this? I know what happened when you found out..." I didn't want to say too much. I didn't want to hurt Evie.

"I don't know what you're talking about." His voice was firm, but not threatening. He also didn't budge.

Why didn't I hear the lie in his words?

Evelyn stepped out from behind him, concern marring her brow as she looked first at Jett and then at me. There was chocolate all over her face and a frown on her lips.

"I don't know what kind of game you're playing, but some...a biker clubhouse isn't any place for a child." I didn't have any legal right to Evie, and it seemed like he wasn't going to give her up. Maybe he actually cared where she ended up and wanted to make sure it wasn't with some whacko, which to be fair, was exactly how I probably seemed. "I've known Evie her whole life. I've been there for her. When you're ready to talk, I'll be here. Staying somewhere..."

"There's a bed and breakfast a block over."

"Well I'll be there, then." I pulled a worn-down business card from my wallet and held it out to Jett.

His fingers brushed mine as he accepted, and a shot of heat flashed across my chest. I sucked in a deep breath. Jett Greyson was *not* my mate. No way. Never.

He slipped the card into his pocket, and I knelt down. "Hey, Evie."

She looked down at her ice cream and then at me. She was still frowning, and I hated if me coming here had made this harder on her. I was trying to do the right thing. I was trying to protect her.

I gave her my business card too, and the stuffed unicorn I'd brought for her.

"You know you can always call me, right?"

She nodded.

"I'll be there as fast as my legs can carry me."

"I know." She smiled, but it didn't reach her glossy eyes.

I wrapped my arms around my best friend's daughter, and I squeezed. I didn't want to let go, but I knew I couldn't just take her. Though I could try to pick her up and run...no.

"I'm not leaving Ashwood without you." I meant it, too.

As I walked away, I noticed a stripe of fudge on my shoulder, a badge from the battle. I lost this round, but I wasn't giving up—even if it meant facing Jett Greyson again.

CHAPTER FIVE

JETT

*B*ittersweet like fine chocolate with a hint of earthiness, Paige's essence remained even as she hurried away. She was tall, almost as tall as me. Her hair was black and straight, her skin a creamy tan. It was her big chestnut eyes and her full lips that filled my head even after she turned. That and the pop of her ass in those loose yet hot-as-fuck pants.

Her strides were long and quick, like she was running late. More likely, it was just a hasty retreat.

I considered the words exchanged, and decided there had to be some kind of miscommunication. I hadn't been a dick, even when she'd tried to take my daughter.

My daughter and *my mate*. I'd found both in one hell of a day, and I still couldn't believe it. My whole life, I'd been alone, and now...

"She hates you."

I looked down at Evelyn, who seemed to have taken a bath in her ice cream. Chocolate was smeared all down the front of her shirt and across half her face. "You think so?"

"Big time."

I turned my attention back to Paige, who was already driving away. "I didn't do anything to her."

"Sometimes you don't have to do something wrong to get in trouble." Evelyn nodded and shook her finger as she spoke.

Sage wisdom from a pipsqueak. "How would you fix it?"

"Oh, that's the easy part." Evelyn smiled. "Tell her you're sorry and give her a hug."

"That might not work as well for me as it does for you."

"You could cry."

I laughed.

She looked at me like she had no idea what was so funny. That was another tool that would work a hell of a lot better for her than it would for me. A ploy I'd have to watch out for now that we were going to be involved in each other's lives. This together thing wasn't going to change. I'd figured out at least. The rest was still a mystery.

The sun was low in the sky. Before long it'd be dark, which meant we needed to go home.

"Let's head back so we don't miss dinner."

"This wasn't dinner?" Evelyn placed her hands on her stomach and looked down. "My tummy's so full."

I had to admit, at her age I would have been thrilled to have ice cream for dinner. And breakfast and lunch, too.

"I'm going to need to eat more than that." I tapped her on the shoulder. "Come on."

The lot was packed when we returned to the clubhouse, so I parked Brick's truck on the street. The sun was setting, casting the world in a soft, ethereal glow. Evelyn ambled out of the passenger side all by herself, fearlessly, just as she had at the doctor's office. With the distance down it was for her, it was quite a feat. She was a tough little squirt, and I admired that.

As we rounded the building, the deep sound of thumping

bass reverberated through the bricks. It wasn't just dinner inside, but a party.

The back door flew open before I reached the handle. Music blared, and the scents of barbeque and booze enveloped me. Home.

A woman fell into my chest—a half-naked, very drunk woman with a big set of fake tits. She giggled and looked up at me, her head leaning on my chest. "O-M-G, I'm so glad you were here to catch me."

Her voice was much too loud. She slid her hand around my neck. She wasn't one of the regulars, but she'd fit right in here.

Before today, I would have slapped her ass and thrown her over my shoulder. Before Paige. Before Evelyn.

I looked down at the kid beside me. Her eyes were wide as a full moon.

Paige was right. This was no place for Evelyn, at least not tonight, not during a party. She looked like she was freaking the hell out, and this was nothing compared to what was likely going on inside.

"Join me, blue eyes," the woman said. "I'll show you a good time."

I gently but firmly removed the woman from my chest.

I turned to Evelyn. "Let's go the other way."

She nodded, but didn't say a thing.

We went back around the building and entered through the business side where our offices were. The music was still loud over here, but everything was dark and empty, and devoid of sex.

I led Evelyn up the staircase. "Sorry you had to see that."

She still didn't say anything.

I flipped the light on in my room, and saw a little pink backpack leaning on the wall by the door. Evelyn ran over and picked it up. Brick must have left her things in here when he passed her off to me.

"Is that all you have?"

She nodded. Her eyes were still wide, and she hugged the stuffed animal Paige had given her. The tough little badass I'd first met was gone, and what remained was a scared little girl who'd lost everything. Shit.

I scanned the room. I hadn't thought this through at all. I had one bed, a single, and a chair. "All right. You get the bed." I looked at the chocolate sauce smeared all over her face. "Shower first. Do you have pajamas in that bag?"

She nodded.

"Good." I showed her the bathroom and how the knob to the shower worked. It was a little wonky, and sputtered if it wasn't turned just so. She just looked at me, and I couldn't tell if she was getting it, so I decided to turn it on for her. I figured when she was done, I'd just turn it back off for her, too, if she needed me to.

"I'm going to go downstairs a minute. I'll be right—"

"Please don't go."

Her lips turned into a tiny frown and my heart broke. "Yeah, okay. I'll be right out in the room. You come on out when you're done, okay?"

"Okay." She nodded.

I grabbed a beer from the mini fridge and settled into my well-worn recliner. It wasn't a bad place to sleep, but we could only do this for so long. Having a kid was forever. Even if we found her mom and shared custody, nothing would ever be the same. I couldn't rely on Brick to lend me his truck forever. And it wasn't fair to make Evelyn see the kind of shit that happened downstairs.

My whole life was about to change, and I hated change. It was hard. Work had been hard switching from doing whatever we got paid for to doing whatever we got paid for *that was within the boundaries of the law.* Sure, I could go out and use my law degree and do something away from the Butchers, but Hawke and Brick, Shaundra, hell, even Ray—they were my family. I didn't mind doing the contracts for the security gigs, or fighting to keep guys from some of the other chapters out of prison. But now I had another family to think about.

Soon after the sounds of water cut off, Evelyn opened the door. Her hair was matted down to her head, and all the chocolate was washed away. She stood there in pink pajamas with unicorns on them, and held tight to both her backpack and her stuffed animal. She looked younger somehow than she had before.

I cleared my throat. "Bed's all yours. Hop on in."

"I don't think I can sleep yet."

"Maybe I could borrow a tablet and you could watch some YouTube."

"Okay." She climbed up and set her bag next to her on the pillow and held tight to her unicorn. "Jett?"

"Yeah."

"You'll come right back, right?"

Broke my heart every fucking time. I smiled at her before heading out into the hall. "I promise."

I expected to have to go down to the party, but Brick was there, leading two women to his bedroom.

"Hey," I said.

"Hey, you have my keys?" Brick narrowed his eyes at me. The women rubbed their hands all over him, vying for his full attention.

"Yeah." I reached into my pocket and held them out.

He didn't take them, and instead clenched his jaw. "You still have the kid?"

"Yep."

39

"Then keep the keys until you get something else worked out."

It wasn't like him to do favors. Maybe he just had a soft spot for kids. "Thanks."

"Oh, don't thank me. I'm taking your bike."

Hell no. No one touched my bike. But then, how was I going to drive Evelyn?

I growled under my breath and said, "Fine."

Brick turned and opened his door. The women ran in and jumped on the bed, stripping off what little clothing they had left.

I nodded toward the women. "They aren't anything like Shaundra."

Brick growled low and fierce. *"Nobody* is like Shaundra."

"Wait." I caught his wrist before he shut the door. "Can I borrow your tablet?"

"Sure, whatever."

He grabbed the device from his dresser and handed it to me. "Don't come back asking for anything else. I'm busy."

Before I could respond, he slammed the door in my face.

Fair enough.

Across the hall, I cracked open the door to my room. Lying in the bed, still holding tight to her unicorn, Evelyn was fast asleep.

* * *

MY EYES SHOT OPEN, to pitch black. My heart threatened to beat out of my chest.

What the hell had startled me? A bad dream? A loud noise?

I blinked hard and my eyes adjusted. There was motion in the bed. Evelyn was tossing and turning.

A shrill screech filled the small room. The kid—the kid

had woken me. I rose from my chair and went to the bedside, unsure what I could do to help her.

"Hey." I touched Evelyn's shoulder.

Her eyes didn't open, but her face squinched up as if she was in pain.

"Evelyn, it's okay. It's just a bad dream, and I'm here."

Her body settled and the stress lines smoothed from her face, leaving her still except for the gentle rise and fall of her chest. I waited there, afraid to take my hand away, afraid she'd wake up or worse, that the nightmare would take over again.

Time passed, and I wasn't sure how much, but it seemed like she was okay. I slid down to the floor, sitting against the wall, with my hand still on her shoulder, and I closed my eyes in search of sleep.

Sliding in and out of consciousness, I found myself dreaming.

Images of big brown eyes, of straight black hair and thick curves, filled my mind. With them were memories of her walking away, frustration that I hadn't made her stay, and undeserved hopes for a future. I'd never given much thought to finding a mate. The kind of women who were worth settling down with weren't the kind I associated with, with the exception of Shaundra. But I didn't think of her like that.

Given a chance with Paige, I was sure to fuck it up. End up like my parents.

Paige. I remembered how she'd glared at me, hands on her wide hips. Before I'd even said a word to her, she hated me. *My mate.*

* * *

MY NOSE BENT under soft pressure. My eyelids were still heavy, but light crept through.

"You shouldn't sleep on the floor, silly."

I opened my eyes and found Evelyn sitting on the edge of the bed, her legs dangling, and her pointer finger aimed at my face.

"You're right," I said. "It was stupid of me."

"You said it, not me."

I nodded and smiled.

Today was the day I'd promised Hawke I'd go to Greenville. I'd expected to wrap up the whole Evelyn thing yesterday, but that was before I knew she was mine. And now, I had no fucking idea what I was doing.

"Go get dressed," I said. "We've got a big day ahead of us."

She grabbed her bag and headed into the bathroom. When she was done, I threw on some deodorant and brushed my teeth. We left the same way we'd entered the clubhouse, through the office side so we didn't end up seeing any naked bodies sprawled out anywhere. I gave myself a mental pat on the back for learning something and not making the same mistake twice. I'd figure this parenting thing out, one day at a time.

A quick stop at a drive-thru for some breakfast on the way, and we both filled our guts before either of us said anything beyond meaningless pleasantries. By that point, we'd reached Greenville City.

There were a shit ton of questions I needed answers to. One bugged me more than the rest. I didn't know what Evelyn was thinking, but I needed to figure out how to press her on the woman who'd ambushed us at the ice cream parlor the day before—my mate.

"Hey squirt, what can you tell me about Paige?"

She turned her whole body toward me. "I don't know."

"You've known her forever, right?"

"Yep."

We approached the Briggs Unlimited tower. I'd scope out

42

the area from afar today, only see what we could see from the truck. It wasn't like I could take the kid inside, so it was a start.

"Was she your neighbor or something?" I asked.

"She used to live with me."

"Oh yeah? You and whoever you were staying with before hanging out with me?"

She turned back around and looked out the window, completely disengaging. "No."

This was dangerous territory. Evelyn's stiff stature and crossed arms made it clear I'd touched a nerve. Something safer—I needed to think of something more comfortable to ask her, or our conversation was over.

We passed the tower. Security wasn't as heavy as I'd expected, at least not from the outside. I decided to park two blocks down to observe the flow of traffic in and out of the building. Here in front of a bank there'd be plenty of cars passing between us and Briggs's tower, plus a decent view of the lot and entrance.

"You have a favorite food?" I asked.

Evelyn looked back over at me and let her hands fall to her lap. "Chocolate."

"That's a good one." This was easier than I'd expected. "Favorite color?"

"Yellow."

"Really? My first guess would have been pink."

She made a sour face.

"But your pajamas are pink." I thought back to the day before. "And your backpack."

"Yeah, but they have *unicorns.*" Her sharp tone made it clear that this was all the explanation that was required.

"Uh-huh." I shifted in my seat. "So unicorns are good, but pink isn't. What about purple?"

"Better. But yellow's the best. Like dandelions." Her eyes

sparkled and she smiled at me. It was the craziest thing, but just one little smile made a warm feeling spread across my chest.

"Or your hair."

"My hair's not—"

The truck jostled. Evelyn threw her hands against the dash, bracing herself, and squealed. I balled my fists, ready to shift, ready to defend my daughter. A man stood in front of the truck, his arms extended over the hood. He lifted a bottle covered in paper and stumbled onto the sidewalk beside us.

"Sorry." He waved from hands and knees.

It was a harmless encounter, but that wasn't the point. My wolf seethed just beneath the surface. It could have been Briggs and his pack. It could have been gunfire instead of a drunk. I was distracted, and that was unacceptable. Evelyn couldn't be here.

I'd fucked up.

I rested my hand on the pocket that held a business card. I needed help. More than anything I wanted that help to come from the woman I knew was my mate, if only I could get her to trust me.

CHAPTER SIX

PAIGE

*M*y article wasn't writing itself no matter how many cups of gritty coffee I picked up downstairs, or how hard I glared at the screen. The bed and breakfast was perfectly nice. The whole damned town seemed perfectly nice. Even Jett had acted reasonable given the fact that I, a total stranger, had tried to steal his kid.

It had been a whole twenty-four hours—nope, twenty-six and a half hours since I'd arrived in town, and the incident went down. Why hadn't they called? Okay, I knew why. But I *really* wanted them to call.

How long was I supposed to sit around in this room waiting? What if Greyson *never* called?

My stomach churned. Maybe it was all the coffee. Maybe I was just getting a little stir-crazy. Either way, it seemed like the perfect time to stretch my legs.

I left my room and headed downstairs. The scent of tuna hit me halfway down, which reminded me of Graybeard, my favorite alley cat. I pulled my phone from my pocket and texted my next door neighbor back home, Mrs. Foster.

P: Hey. Wanted to make sure you remembered to feed the cat.

F: Of course. Don't worry. Have fun on your trip.

FUN? Yeah, right. But she didn't know why I was here or what I was dealing with. I didn't really want to text it to her, either.

P: Thanks!

THERE. Perfect.

"Joining us for dinner, Paige?"

I looked up and found the lady from the desk. Mrs. Something...I couldn't remember her name. She had her gray hair up in a tight bun, and her squinted eyes made me think she desperately needed glasses. She had the look of a television librarian. Not the hot, lets her hair down and then she's gorgeous kind, but the normal kind.

"Yeah, I, uh." Dinner...ugh. My stomach growled and twisted. I couldn't eat. "Do you have any crackers?"

"I have rolls."

"I'd love a roll."

She disappeared into the dining area and I stood a moment, unsure if I was supposed to follow or wait here. As soon as I took a few steps after her, she returned, with bread on a little plate with flowers painted on it.

She smiled at me, but if I wasn't mistaken there was a sadness there. Was...was I supposed to sit down to eat with her? No. Pleasing other people wasn't my job. I had two jobs while in town—

Evie, and writing.

"Thank you." I headed back up the steps and plopped down on the bed with my roll and my laptop and read the start of my article.

Screw stiff jeans. Gimme comfort. Gimme a pair of palazzos paired with a crop top and

NOT SO GOOD. Maybe bad writing was better than no writing. Start getting the creative juices flowing and magic would happen.

I like pants. I like comfortable pants.

I TOOK a bite of the bread and considered what else I could write.

I like bread, too.

IT WAS TERRIBLE, ridiculously atrocious, and not at all what I wanted to write. What I wanted to share was the image that appeared in my head every time I closed my eyes. I wanted to write a ballad of adoration for the tight white t-shirt that perfectly showcased biceps the size of my thighs, that stretched across broad shoulders and his thick and tapered chest. I wanted to know the feel of those firm pecs and sculpted abs beneath my palms, instead of just guessing what it would be like based on the impact of my face when I'd crashed into Jett fucking Greyson. And I wanted to feel all these things about someone else. Anyone other than that lying, cheating, no good—

My phone buzzed and tickled my thigh.

I hopped out of the bed, grateful for the distraction, and hit accept. It was probably Janie wondering where the hell my article was.

"Hello."

"Paige?" Holy hell, it was him. That deep rumbly voice shot excitement through my entire body like he'd reached through the phone and run the pad of his thumb across my ear.

"Yes. Who is this?" No question, I knew it was Mr. Sexy Ink, but I could pretend to be not desperate. There was no lie for him to detect, even if an untruth was implied.

"It's Jett. We started off on the wrong foot. I'd like to remedy that."

"I think we started just fine." Okay, *that* was a lie.

There was a rustle of movement on the other side of the line. I imagined him smoothing his hand over his rough beard, up through his brown hair, his eyes flashing with something not quite readable.

"We should get together and do this in person."

Don't seem desperate. Don't be too eager. "Do what?"

"I need your help." He paused. "With Evelyn."

Hell yes, the ball was back in my court...or in my court for the first time. "That's why I'm in Ashwood."

"Great. I'll pick you up in twenty minutes."

"Twenty—" Uhhhhhh. "Yeah, great." Totally great.

48

"See you then."

The line clicked, but I was still standing there like an idiot. And then I realized I was getting what I wanted—a chance to see Evie, make sure she was okay. I'd convince Jett to send her home where she belonged, where she could see her friends and resume her normal life. As much as that was possible. He needed my help because he wasn't equipped to be a father, no surprise there.

Parenting wouldn't be easy for me, either, I was sure. But it wouldn't be forever. Linda would get better, and I'd be there to hold the pieces together until then.

So what was I supposed to wear to give the appearance of someone put together enough to take care of a kid, and also prudish enough not to give Jett the wrong impression? Sure, I felt the undeniable draw that *had* to be the mating instinct, but there was no reason to believe he felt the same way. He couldn't. I couldn't. I had to be wrong. This was *Jett Greyson*.

I dug through my bag and reminded myself of all the reasons he wasn't the guy for me. He abandoned my best friend when she was pregnant *with his baby.* That was cause enough never to touch the man. I didn't need more. I'd save all the other reasons for later, for when he was looking at me and my legs turned to jelly.

I put on my long-sleeved green dress and looked in the mirror. Sure, there was some shoulder showing, but the cut was high, so no cleavage. But my legs...too much leg. I threw on some leggings underneath and decided I looked generally acceptable. The only thing better would have been if I'd brought along my Victorianesque coat, the one with buttons all the way up to my chin, but I hadn't packed it, so this was going to have to do. Also, it was summer. So, the coat would have been overkill, anyway. This whole dress and pants at the same time thing I had going on—totally acceptable.

There was a rapid succession of taps at my bedroom

door. Had it already been twenty minutes? It felt like five. Maybe it was five and he was just screwing with me in some sadistic mind game.

I shook the thought. It was fine. Everything was fine. It probably wasn't even Jett at the door. He didn't seem like a gentle knocker, more of a pounder, hard...strong...

"Just a minute," I called, then headed over and opened the door.

Standing in the hall with a wide grin was the woman from the desk. She wore the kind of smile that took over her entire face. She owned the place, so it was going to get more awkward if at some point I didn't remember her name. Maybe it started with an A. That sounded right. Althea? Alethea? Amy?

"Paige, there's a gentleman downstairs for you."

"Thanks." I smiled and I closed the door behind me before heading down the hall. My nerves had me both wanting to run to him and wanting to run away.

Once I was down the steps, I waited for his scent to greet me, but it didn't. He wasn't there. I glanced around the entry and living room areas, and then figured the only other place he could be was outside.

So, I turned the handle and stepped out. The last shreds of sunlight were like high beams pointed right in my face. It was possible I'd spent too much time inside with the curtains shut.

I stepped down from the porch, shielding my eyes like some kind of cave-dwelling bat, and blinked hard. An engine purred nearby, loud and smooth like a motorcycle, and the scent of warm spiced cider greeted me. I was almost afraid to move my hand and look, because I knew right there by the curb, it had to be Jett.

Sucking it up like a damned adult, I lowered my hand, and there he was—leather jacket covering another t-shirt, this time a gray one. I practically drooled. I had never been much for leather, but this man could make me appreciate the finer points of wearing a potato sack. And, it made my choice in long sleeves seem more appropriate in the moderate evening air.

"Hey," he said. Damn that voice.

"Hey."

Wait, he wasn't expecting me to ride with him on the bike, was he?

"I can follow you in my car," I said.

His lips curved in a smirk that I knew was at my expense. He reached out, offering me a helmet.

This was crazy. I couldn't ride a motorcycle. Where was I supposed to put my hands? I took the helmet and put it on, knowing it was my lady parts making this decision and not my brain. The fierce bear inside me was rolling over for him, submitting, waiting for him to rub her belly...and that was exactly what I wanted to do, too.

Against my better judgement, I climbed on behind him and grabbed onto the sides of the seat, hoping it would be enough to keep me from falling and becoming roadkill once he started driving.

His masculine scent enveloped me and I tried like hell to lean back far enough that I wasn't touching him. I could feel the heat of the engine, the heat of his body. And the seat rumbled in delicious torture.

Jett looked back over his shoulder at me. "You have to hold on."

"I am. I have a great grip...on this little metal thing here by the seat."

"You have to hold onto *me*." He reached back and grabbed my wrists. My breath caught in my chest as a hot slice of electricity shot up my arms. He pulled my wrists forward, with firm but gentle pressure, and I didn't fight him. He pulled me against him and placed my arms over his chest.

I was either grinning from ear to ear, or again drooling—definitely one or the other—as I grabbed hold of his jacket. I wanted to stretch my palms beneath the leather, but I didn't.

When my body was flush against his, the motorcycle began to move. I held my breath, terrified that I'd fall off. I squeezed my fists so hard I was sure my knuckles were white, and I leaned my cheek on his back. The leather was cool and pleasant against my face, and I closed my eyes. It was a strange combination of sensations and emotions.

"Doing okay?" he asked.

"Mm-hmm, great." Yep, that was a lie, or at least kind of. I was excited but scared. And I was turning into a big fat liar, just in time to hang out with a shifter, the only kind of guy who could sense the difference.

"I'll go slow," he said.

It didn't feel slow. The wind whipped my hair, but I could see everything we passed, unlike being a passenger staring straight out the car window. When we went around a turn, everything shifted a bit to the side, but not enough to make me feel like I was falling. And after the second turn, I started to enjoy the feeling of riding on this thing. But all too soon, Jett slowed the bike and parked on the side of the street.

We were sitting in front of a little restaurant marked Big Tony's, and only after we both climbed off did I think to ask something I should have thought of as soon as he'd arrived on the bike.

"So is Evie waiting for us with a friend?" I followed him up to the door, which he opened for me.

"She's with a friend." Something about the way he said that set off my bullshit alarm. It wasn't a lie, but...

"Hey, Jett." A round guy with a sauce-stained apron waived to us as we entered.

"Hey, Tony." Jett did one of those bro nods, which was more of a chin lift, then he led me between red and white checkered tables like he knew where we were going. Maybe Evie was at the last table and he could see her already digging into a slice of pizza.

"We *are* going to see her now, right?"

I knew the answer without him having to say a damned thing, yet still I was stupid enough to hope I was wrong.

"Take a seat." He gestured to a chair at an empty table, where there was absolutely no sign of Evie.

"What is this?" My palms stung as my fingernails dug into my palms. "Jett?"

"It's dinner," he said.

"I thought...you know what? This is *not* what I agreed to. I'm..." If I left, that was it. I couldn't expect him to hand over my best friend's daughter if I stormed off now. What happened to proving I was a responsible caregiver? Ugh, sometimes I hated when my brain told me to be reasonable.

"Please." He gestured to the chair.

I sat down, even though I didn't want to. I felt like an idiot. I'd jumped on the back of his bike, no questions asked, and my sanity went all haywire with a touch or when he spoke. That was the solution—he couldn't touch me and he had to write down everything he wanted to say, so I could read it without losing myself in his deep voice or those gorgeous blue pools of his eyes. Was that too much to ask?

He sat across from me, and I didn't stare. I was too mad at myself to appreciate the view, anyway.

"Where is Evie?" My tone was cold, but I didn't care. I crossed my arms and stood my ground.

"Like I said, she's with a friend. I needed us to be alone."

Sure, that sounded hot. I wanted to be alone, and tangled up naked with him, but I wasn't going to do that, and not just because he'd knocked up and betrayed my friend. He was a bad person, a criminal, a manipulative bastard.

"This isn't a date," I said.

His brows shot up. "It wasn't intended to be."

Oh. My cheeks grew hot.

He continued, "Like I said on the phone, I need your help. With Evelyn. I thought we could get to know each other—"

"Sounds like a date to me."

His lips flattened into a line. I was frustrating him. Good.

"You care about Evelyn," he said.

It didn't sound like a question, but I treated it like one anyway. "Yes."

"So do I. Do you trust me?"

"Hell no." I shot him a look that said everything my words didn't, though to be honest, I'd been pretty clear what I thought of him with my words already.

"So how do you expect me to trust you if we don't get to know each other?" he asked.

Okay, maybe that was fair. Tension eased from my shoulders and I laced my fingers together in my lap. But I was still on edge, ready to fight if I needed to.

"What do you want to know?"

"Everything." He leaned forward, placing an elbow on the table.

I let myself stare at his lips only for a second, then I met his gaze with steel. "How about something more specific to start."

"Last time I asked this, you seemed offended when I didn't know the answer already."

Uh oh, here we go. Round two. I just stared at him and waited.

"I've thought a lot about it, and Evelyn doesn't want to talk, so I really need to ask you again."

Ask me *what* exactly? What did he ask her that he needed to ask me? "Okay, what?"

"You said you were friends with Marla. Who is Marla?"

This time I wasn't surprised, but the fact that he didn't know still left a bad taste in my mouth.

The big guy that worked there came over, and with a wave from Jett, he turned right back around.

"She was my best friend. She was Evie's mom." My voice cracked, but I was holding my shit together pretty well if I did say so myself.

"Tell me about her."

"She looked just like Evelyn, with that blond hair and big smile, and she was human. She was hilarious and sweet, and we were best friends since forever. You met her at a coffee-house where she worked."

He looked down at the table, and I could see the gears turning in his head. When he looked up at me again, his eyes were soft. "Big brown eyes, always at Big Beans on Friday mornings?"

"Yes. That was her." Finally, he remembered.

His brows furrowed. "You've been speaking about her in the past tense."

"Yeah, she died. It's been a couple of years now."

"I'm sorry for your loss." He wore a gentle expression like he was fucking sincere. I knew for a fact he wasn't lying, because of the whole shifter thing. This whole thing was weird. It was hard to hate him when he was being so nice about it all.

"Thanks." I grabbed the straw from the table and picked at the paper.

"What happened to Evelyn after that?"

"She moved in with her grandmother. Everything was fine. Tough, but fine, for a long time. I visit every couple of months, and do what I can when Marla's mom calls needing something." I looked at him, and he seemed to have no recognition to any of this. "So when Marla's mom broke her hip in a fall…"

"That's how she ended up here." His lips flattened into a line and he laced his fingers together on the edge of the table.

"Yeah."

"I wish I would have known sooner."

"What?"

"About Evelyn. I was in a shitty place for—"

"What do you mean, wish you had known? Known that it was hard on Marla's mom? Or that Marla struggled to raise Evelyn by herself?" Frustration boiled just beneath the surface, and I didn't care that we were in public. Jett needed to hear just how much shit he'd left Marla to deal with by herself. Hot damn, this man was a rollercoaster.

"I wish I'd known I had a daughter."

That left me floored. I stared at him, knowing I hadn't heard a lie in his words. How the fuck was that the truth?

"Marla told you when she found out. She told you and you sent her away." My eyes glossed and my voice broke.

"No." He leaned forward. "I wish she had, but she didn't. I never knew."

I stared at him, as he spoke the truth. I sat still and stunned as my world turned upside down.

CHAPTER SEVEN

JETT

*T*he most beautiful woman I'd ever laid eyes on sat across from me, trying to figure out if the hatred she felt for me was just. I couldn't blame her. I'd committed my fair share of sins and then some, but this was not one of them.

"I don't..." Paige frowned, and a small crease formed on her forehead. "Why would she lie to me about that?"

"I have no idea." I remembered the flirty woman from the coffeehouse, but we hadn't known each other beyond a first name basis. We'd shared an awkward one night stand, and after that, I'd started buying my coffee elsewhere.

"If Marla didn't tell you about Evie, what else did she tell me that wasn't true? I should have known if she was lying to me."

"I wish I could tell you." Sure, shifters could sense lies, but not necessarily omissions of truth or deception through carefully chosen words. If Paige hadn't expected her friend to lie to her, she wouldn't have been looking for deception.

Paige put her hands on the table and stared down at them. I wanted to reach across and touch her. I wanted to console her, but we weren't at a place with each other where I could do that. I needed to give her space.

Paige looked up at me. "How many times did you two…"

"One night, six or seven years ago."

"She did say it was just one date before you started ghosting her. So at least that's consistent." A line formed between her brows. "And it was eight years ago. Evelyn is seven."

Paige gave me a disapproving glare that told me I should know how old my kid was. She had given me a lot of those glares, but this time, she was right.

"I did ask her how old she was," I offered in my defense.

"She didn't tell you?"

"No." I sucked in a deep breath. "She's hardly told me anything. But I want her to. I want to be the father she deserves."

"You can't do that." Her eyes narrowed and then softened. "You can't do that *here*. With your—"

She leaned in closer and her sweet scent enveloped me. "With your biker gang."

Her words stung.

"We're not a gang." I maintained my posture and my tone, not letting my discomfort show. "We're a motorcycle club."

"Yeah, well, I've seen Sons of Anarchy."

I laughed. It sounded a little bitter, but really, I was just amused. She blinked hard and sat up straight. I admired the single freckle on her cheek, the thickness of her eyelashes, the curve of her breasts.

"We do security," I said. "It's a good show, but how many times could an MC really sell guns to the same gang? They must have thrown out their assault weapons every time they needed a new clip."

A hint of a smile played on her lips. It made her even more beautiful. I wanted to taste those full lips, see the way they looked wrapped around my cock, my fingers threaded through her silky hair.

"Okay, so what Marla told me about that part of your life is also untrue."

"Sort of. The Butchers used to be...for hire." I wasn't proud of it, but it was true.

"Like hitmen?" she whispered.

"Not exactly. But it's different now."

"Even if you guys are good now, what's to stop trouble from coming home with you, to Evie?"

I wished I had a good answer. It's a big part of why I was here, asking for help.

"I would do anything to protect her." *Or you.* I left the last part unspoken. This woman was my mate, and I'd do anything to make her mine, but for now I'd settle on her being able to look at me without disapproval.

A sound came from across the table, a groan from her stomach. She blushed and looked away.

"We should order," I said.

"Yeah, okay." She grabbed a menu from next to the napkin holder.

Her lips moved the tiniest bit as she read the paper card. It was adorable.

Paige flicked her gaze up and looked at me. "What?"

"Nothing."

She narrowed her eyes and then leaned back. "What's good here?"

"The pizza, the lasagna, the chicken with—"

"Back up. I haven't had lasagna in forever."

I gave a wave to Tony, and he came right over.

"Ready to order?" He smiled at both of us, his attention lingering just a little too long on my mate. The growl that came from my chest caught me by surprise. I'd never been one for jealousy, but I'd also never found my mate before.

The wolf in me was ready to tear this man to shreds just for looking at her—again completely unexpected. And I liked Tony.

Both Tony and Paige stared at me like I was crazy. Hell, I couldn't blame them.

Better to order and then we'd be alone again. "We'll both have the lasagna."

I watched Paige's expression change from surprise to something else. Her breathing quickened ever so slightly as her eyes grazed over my chest, then she shook her head and looked away. Maybe she liked that I was being territorial.

It wasn't just me who felt this draw. But did she feel the same certainty I did that we were meant to be mates? Plenty of women had looked at me like that, but I'd never felt this way about anyone before.

"What would you two like to drink?" Tony asked, this time keeping his attention set on me. Smart man.

"Water for me. Paige?"

"Water's great." She looked at the brick wall beside us, down at the checkerboard table, anywhere but at me. I wanted to grab her chin and force her to look at me. Taste her lips and see what she had to say then.

Tony left, and I decided to test my luck. I reached across the table and touched her hand.

Paige snapped her gaze to mine, and her pupils dilated.

She was soft, and warm, and she didn't pull away. With just a simple touch, I could scent her desire, and my cock grew hard.

I asked, "Where were we?"

"Marla." Paige sucked in a deep breath and pulled away. "We were talking about my friend, your baby mama. And how you're not equipped to give Evie everything she needs."

"Right."

"What school is she going to attend? Where is she going to sleep?"

I hadn't considered school. I guessed seven was old enough for that. When did they start, five or six? "I gave her my bed last night."

"Sure," Paige said. "But what about tomorrow or the next day? What about a year from now? Ten? You can't have her sharing a room with you at your clubhouse forever."

That was fair. Evelyn did need more, and she deserved to have it. And the more I heard about her situation, the more permanent it seemed to be.

My first thought was my parents' cabin. It was outside of town, nestled in the forest, just far enough away to be able to shift in privacy. I hadn't been to the house in years, and hadn't planned on going back. Shit, for all I knew—for all I'd cared—the roof could have caved in by now. I'd intended to let it rot, and my childhood memories with it.

"You're right," I said. "Of course you're right. But now I'm just trying to figure out how to get through one day at a time. I will figure out how to make this work."

Paige studied me, and her expression softened. "You really want to be there for her, don't you?"

I didn't have to think about my answer. "Yes."

Since I'd found out Evelyn was mine, hell even before I knew for sure, I knew she was a part of me. She was mine, and I would do anything for her.

Paige sighed. "Then I guess...I'm going to help you."

Her tone made it clear that this wasn't her first choice, but whether she was reluctant or not, I needed her help.

Tony set down two plates in front of us, mountains of noodles, cheese, and red sauce, before heading back to the kitchen.

I'd come into this diner not knowing if I could trust Paige. After only a short time, though, I knew. She cared for my daughter enough to help me, and enough not to run away with her. I could count on Paige.

She dug into her food, and while I ate, I watched her. Some people ate merely to survive. This woman enjoyed it, though. She made the most delicious noises of appreciation as the lasagna slid down her throat. I watched the way she closed her eyes and savored the flavors as they rolled over her tongue. Shamelessly, I wondered what other faces she made in pleasure.

When we finished eating, I made a mental note to feed her as often as she'd let me. I insisted that I be the one to pay. She only protested once. And when we left, I wished it wasn't time to head back yet.

This time when we climbed on my bike, she melted into me without hesitation. Her soft curves enveloped me, and it was hard as fuck to pay attention to anything but the feel of her. I pulled up to the bed and breakfast, wishing I could take her home with me.

But the progress we'd made tonight was fragile, and the stakes were too high. I couldn't fuck up with Paige.

She climbed off first, and I followed her up to the door. I felt like a damned teenager, palms sweating, my gut fluttering, waiting to see if she'd let me steal a kiss.

"You never did tell me what you needed my help with." Paige's soft smile lit her big brown eyes. Her sleek black hair shimmered in the moonlight, and I found myself unable to stop staring at her luscious lips.

"I wanted to ask if you'd help me by watching Evelyn tomorrow."

"And you had to take me out to dinner for that?"

Her lips quirked up to one side, making an adorable dimple. She was so fucking perfect—curves and sass, gorgeous and cute. "I needed to make sure I could trust you first. I just found out I had a daughter. I didn't want to risk someone trying to take her away."

She cringed. "Sorry about that."

"Even if that person is my mate."

She sucked in a sharp breath. "You think I'm your mate?"

Hell, I'd already put myself out there. Time to go for it. "I know you are."

"And what if I say no?"

I took a step closer, testing the boundaries. Her heartbeat quickened and her pupils dilated ever so slightly. The sweet scent of her desire mingled with her earthy essence, and I knew she wanted me as much as I wanted her. "You already said yes."

"I'm pretty sure I didn't." She didn't move back as I leaned in so close that we were almost touching. With her on the step, we were the same height, eye to eye.

"You told me you'd help with Evelyn. So you'll watch her for me tomorrow, won't you?"

"Yes, but I thought you meant—"

I reached up and brushed her cheek with my fingertips. Soft, smooth, the feel of her skin was a drug and I was hooked. She leaned into my touch and exhaled slowly, and her eyes fluttered shut.

She felt it. No question she felt the same instinct I did. The need to fuck, the need to mate, the need to claim her as mine.

She leaned closer to me and tilted her chin up. "Jett."

Soft and searing, I claimed her lips with mine. She was supple, sweet, and so fucking intoxicating. My cock throbbed against my fly, and I needed to claim her right here on the doorstep.

I ran my fingers through her hair, and she arched her back, leaning into me. Everything else melted away, everything but Paige.

She reached around me, her arms exploring my shoulders, my back. Her lips parted, offering more, letting me in deep. More. I wanted more.

The door opened behind her. I didn't care, but Paige did. She pulled back, her cheeks flushed.

"I, uh...that was..." She bit her lip and smiled at the same time. The way she looked up at me through her lashes, it seemed she was shy, which only made me more desperate to have her.

"Coming in?" The little woman in the doorway put her hand on her hip.

Paige laughed. "I am. He's going home."

"Good night, Paige." I took her hand and gave her one last kiss, this time on her knuckles.

"Good night."

She went inside and I shamelessly admired the way her hips swayed, the way her waist cut in, and the fine roundness of her ass.

Mine.

The gray-haired woman looked me up and down, smiled, and shut the door in my face without another word. And I was left thinking about everything that had happened, the dinner, the kiss. I hadn't wanted the night to end. I'd wanted to tear Paige's clothes off. It felt like Paige had wanted that, too. Besides the nasty case of blue balls I was definitely going to have after this, I couldn't have asked for a better night. Paige was worth the wait.

* * *

AFTER DINNER, my plan had been to return to the clubhouse. Instead, I found myself driving in the opposite direction. I caught a glimpse of a future I'd never thought possible, one I'd never thought much about until now—a family of my own. And that possible future had me thinking about my past.

The summer heat of the day was long gone, leaving the air brisk. Each inhale filled my lungs with a refreshing sting, while each exhale billowed like smoke. Paved roads gave way to loose stone, then dirt. Out here was shitty terrain for my bike, but the secluded forest was perfect for wolves and bears. It's why my father had chosen this place. And it's why I returned.

I passed the treehouse where Hawke and I used to play, the stream where we used to splash to escape summer heat. Those memories were the best I had of this place. The rest were...not as pleasant.

The trees broke apart enough for me to see the little log cabin in the clearing up ahead. Moonlight shone down on the building, and I parked my bike at the edge of the drive.

I sat there longer than I needed to, looking over the building.

Staring at the porch, I imagined a kid version of me curled up by the door waiting for hours to be allowed back inside. Beside that was the window that my father had shattered with a kitchen chair.

After they'd died, I'd thought about torching the place, set a match or ten and watch it burn. But I hadn't. Instead, I'd left it to rot. Maybe letting the place stand hadn't been a mistake.

I thought about Evelyn, and wondered how she was doing. I pulled out my phone and dialed Brick.

"Jett." He answered on the first ring, his voice sounding pained.

"What's wrong?"

"It's your kid..."

Fuck. I shouldn't have trusted him. If he let her get hurt—

"She's a monster." In the background, there was laughter, high-pitched, maniacal laughter.

"She's okay?"

"Of course *she's* okay. You need to get back here before she rips out all of my arm hair. She thinks it's funny."

Because it *was* funny. That was my daughter. "Good talk," I said. "Thanks again, Brick."

"Get back here right now, you motherfucking shit-for-brains—"

Content that Evelyn was fine, I hung up.

As soon as I slid my phone into my pocket, it buzzed. Expecting it to be Brick, I checked the number just in case. It was Hawke.

"Yeah?" I answered.

"Give me good news." His tone was more misery than command.

I'd promised to deal with the Greenville City Pack, and I had let personal business get in the way. Juggling responsibilities was new territory for me. "I'm going for a meeting tomorrow."

"I'm counting on you, Jett."

"I won't let you down."

The line clicked. And I only hoped I could deliver. Evelyn would be safe, so I could focus on Briggs. But that was for tomorrow. Tonight, I had different plans.

I climbed off my bike and waded through the overgrown grass toward the cabin. My jaw ached with how hard it was clenched. Each step was harder than the last, like my legs were made of lead. When I reached the door, I knew I could still turn back. For a moment, I considered it.

Just as quickly as the thought had struck, I discarded it, and turned the knob.

For Paige. For Evelyn.

Stale air and dust escaped into the night, a cloud reentering the world after being trapped without circulation for a decade in a wooden box.

I hit the switch by the door, but the power was out. No surprise there. Still, I could see well enough to make out the fireplace and the ugly yellow sofa where my dad used to pass out drunk. I could see my mother's framed needlework that had once been on the wall, before my father had discarded it on the floor. There was as much shattered glass on the carpet as there was carpet. Home sweet home.

One day, maybe I could say that and actually mean it. After a hell of a lot of work, maybe the dark cloud of my past would fade, rewritten by new memories of a better future.

CHAPTER EIGHT

JETT

*B*rick had been a dick when I'd returned to the clubhouse. To be fair, I had left my kid with him longer than I'd said. He was pissy, but he'd get over it.

Evelyn bounced on the bench seat, her attention darting to and fro over the truck's dash. After a better night of sleep, she was starting the day with a beaming smile and more energy than she'd had the day before. Seeing that she was happy took the edge off my nerves for the upcoming mission.

"What do you think we're going to do today, me and Paige?" Her tone was jovial, and she squeezed her little arms around her stuffed unicorn.

At least one of us was in a good mood. "I don't know, squirt. What do you like to do, besides eating ice cream?"

"That's a great idea. Yes! We *have* to get ice cream." A twinkle of mischief played in her bright blue eyes. "It was *your* idea."

I laughed. "Okay, but what else?"

"I like to draw, and I like to play outside."

I pictured Evelyn standing in the doorway to the treehouse

Hawke and I had built as kids, dirt smudged on her face. She would love the cabin. I just had to get it ready for her, and in watching her giddiness, I'd learn to love the cabin, too.

"Do you like the woods?" I raised a brow and shot her a glance.

"Maybe."

"Maybe?" What kind of answer was that? Was she being coy?

"Yeah, maybe. What's it like?"

She'd never been to the woods at all? If she used to live in the city, I guessed that made sense. But shifters weren't meant to live in concrete and exhaust. Nature was in our DNA.

"You're in for a treat. There are trees everywhere, perfect for climbing. There's a stream to play in, and squirrels to chase."

"I'd like to see that."

Sure, I'd missed a hell of a lot of firsts, but this one was mine. I was glad to share it with her. "I'll take you."

"Today. After you pick me up."

Today? I couldn't promise that. "I'm not sure what time I'll get back."

"I don't mind, really. It can be the middle of the night."

I looked at her. She looked completely serious, and I guessed this was why seven-year-olds didn't make their own rules.

"What? I don't need to sleep."

"Maybe. I don't want to make any promises about today."

"Okay." She frowned and looked down at the unicorn in her lap.

I hated to disappoint her. "I will take you soon. I can promise that."

She nodded, but her whole body sagged in defeat.

I parked the truck on the curb in front of the bed and breakfast. As I climbed out, I noticed the door to the building open.

Out stepped Paige, in yoga pants and a t-shirt. She looked like a different person than she had the night before, completely at ease, and with her hair in wild curls. I liked it. I liked her in a dress or in pants, with straight hair or curly. I just liked her.

"Hey." She waved to me, then knelt down to hug the ball of energy running straight for her.

Evelyn threw her arms around Paige, and I watched a smile take over my mate's face.

This was my family. I didn't just have Hawke and the Butchers anymore. I had Paige and Evelyn. But I still had a lot of work to do before I could be the kind of father and mate that they deserved.

Paige stood and looked to me. "Any idea what time you'll be back?"

"With any luck, before dinner. I'll call if my meeting runs late." But I wasn't just hoping the meeting didn't run late. I was hoping *to get* a meeting. Peace was riding on it.

Something flashed in Paige's big brown eyes, and just as quickly as I noticed it, it was gone. "Be careful."

"I'll be fine. Don't worry."

She stared at me, unblinking. What was I supposed to say to convince her?

My footing faltered as Evelyn slammed into me and wrapped her arms around my legs. I hadn't expected the hug, and I wasn't quite sure what to do.

She said, "Don't forget what you promised."

She smiled up at me, and I realized, that was the kind of face that was impossible to say no to. Given that she was bright, I was sure she already knew how to use that to her advantage. I was in over my head in every fucking aspect of my life.

I patted her back. "I won't."

"All right, munchkin, let him go." Paige ushered Evelyn back up to the door.

"Stay out of trouble." I waved and climbed back into the driver's seat.

Evelyn kept on waving as I drove away, and for the first time, I could see myself in a domestic role. The father, the provider, leaving for work. Leaving his woman, his kid.

For the first time, I wasn't looking forward to the next mission, but to returning home.

* * *

I PARKED on the street two blocks from the Briggs tower. If this meeting went to hell, it was better not to have Brick's truck, my only way of escape, trapped in the enemy's lot.

As I walked up to the tall tower, I noted the lack of security at the door. Given Briggs appeared to be a businessman, in addition to being an aggressive pack's alpha, I'd expected at least one or two guards.

I fiddled with my cufflinks, wishing jeans were appropriate for this kind of shit. Show up looking like a biker, and I'd never make it to Briggs.

Inside, the lobby was empty save for a sharp-faced woman behind the reception desk. Her scent said wolf, which would make our conversation easier. I slid my hands into my pockets and approached. "I need to speak to Mr. Briggs."

The receptionist devoured me with her eyes. "You really should have called first. Mr. Briggs is booked up at least two months out."

"He'll make time to see me."

"And why is that?"

I leaned forward and spoke softly, sure that she could hear me. "If I leave here empty-handed, there will be war."

She bolted up in her chair, and her breathing hitched. She believed me. Good.

When she spoke, her voice was higher and softer than it had been. "Take a seat and I'll see what I can do."

"Thank you." I gave her a nod and took a seat across the lobby, one with a view of both the entry and the elevators.

I missed most of what she said into the phone, but I didn't need to know. My message had been delivered, and Briggs *would* clear his schedule to meet with me. No alpha would risk overlooking a threat to his pack.

It didn't take long before a big guy in a suit came out of the elevator. He had black hair and the kind of hard, smashed face that said he was born for MMA. The way he held himself told me all I needed to know. This guy was security, the kind I'd expected when I'd arrived. He scanned the lobby, eyes narrowed. I headed over, knowing it was me he was looking for. When he finally noticed me, he went stiff as a board, with his hand on his belt.

He didn't need a weapon. I was only here to talk. I'd make that clear sooner rather than later, assure him there was no need for violence.

"Mr...?" He further narrowed his eyes, squinting so far that his green irises practically disappeared.

"Greyson." I offered my card.

The guard took and looked it over before shoving it in his pocket. "Come with me, please."

"Of course." I followed him into the elevator.

When the doors clicked shut, he put a key in.

"Spread 'em."

I did as he said, and accepted the pat-down as standard.

"Are you in charge?" I asked.

"New head of security. What do you want, lawyer?"

This would go one of two ways. I could answer or not. Either way, I risked never reaching the Greenville pack alpha. Better to put forth a good faith effort and hope that intention was reciprocated.

"We need to discuss what happened with the Silent Butchers. I'm here for peaceful discussion."

The guard looked me over, then nodded. Seemingly appeased, he pushed a series of buttons. The elevator went down instead of up. My best guess—pack business was done in the basement, hidden from those working in the offices above.

The doors opened, revealing a long hall. The guard gestured for me to exit first.

I took a step forward, and as I did, the hair on the back of my neck stood on end. A sense of dread rushed through me, and I turned...just in time for a needle to stab me in the neck.

* * *

Everything was black.

My limbs felt like stone, stiff and heavy. I tried to force my eyes open, but I couldn't tell if they were working. Every thought, every motion was delayed. What had that asshole injected me with?

The ground beneath me jostled...no, it wasn't the ground. I was on a hard surface, hard and *moving*—the trunk of a car.

When we arrived wherever we were going, my life would be forfeit unless I put up a fight. I needed this chemical shit out of my system. Now. My best chance to quicken that process was to shift.

I focused on the wolf inside of me, called him to the surface.

My bones cracked and fur sprouted all over my body.

Transformation was my salvation, and it was fucking working. The fog cleared, replaced by rabid, raging fury.

There wasn't space to rise to my feet, but I sure as hell was going to do what I could to be ready when that trunk opened. I tore at my suit shirt with my fangs, fighting to free myself from the constraints of my clothing.

The car turned, and I slid to the side, crashing into the wall of the trunk. And with another abrupt jostle, the car stopped. The rumble of the engine remained, so it was unclear whether this was a temporary stop or our final destination.

The floor shifted slightly and metal slammed against metal. Heavy footsteps approached.

I poised myself to lunge. This was it—fight or die.

There was a pop, and a thread of light peeked through the seal. The trunk opened, and I dove.

Tearing through flesh, I sank my teeth into the shoulder of the nearest body. Hot metallic fluid filled my mouth and tinged my tongue. I flexed my claws into his skin, assuring my hold.

A pained wail vibrated through the man's chest.

He grabbed the back of my neck, digging his fingers into me until the pain faded to numbness. He stumbled and flailed, trying to tear me from my hold, fueling me to clamp down harder.

A jolt stabbed into my back, piercing electric prods. It was enough of a shock to allow the man to pull me off, enough for him to throw me to the ground. My side hit stone and dirt, and I struggled to rise to my feet.

The shock came again, and again—a cow prod. How had I not realized there were two men? Neither shifted. They didn't have to. Between shocks, they kicked me. The constant assault made it hard to move.

"Fuck, Tiny. You're bleeding bad."

Tiny, the one from the elevator, grunted in response.

The assault stopped, a short reprieve. I could hardly breathe because of the agonizing pain stabbing in my chest. My ribs were broken, no question, and who the hell knew what else.

My best chance was to run. I had to run.

The two men faced each other, and I couldn't hear what they were saying beyond the pounding of my pulse in my ears.

I had to move or I would die.

So I ran—I ran like hell.

CHAPTER NINE

PAIGE

"*A*unt Paaaaaaige, I'm bored." Evie rolled over on the sticky vinyl cushion and looked up at me.

It was understandable. We'd been at the library for a few hours, and I was getting tired of sitting, too.

"Which book was your favorite?"

She lifted her head and knocked over the pile of hard-covers beside her. "This one." She held up a book with a cartoonish unicorn on it and beamed at me, her hair wild and unruly.

"What's it called?"

"Surfing on a Rainbow."

"Sounds fun. What did you like about it?"

"It's funny. It has rainbow farts."

I just looked at her, thinking I had to have heard her wrong.

"And sparkles."

"Did you finish all of it?"

"Mm-hmm." She nodded. "But I want to take it home. Can I? Can I, please?"

She had the adorable pouty face down pat. She'd upped her game since our last visit back home.

"Sure." The next thing I knew, I was getting a library card in a town I didn't live in, one I'd expected to hate. Ashwood wasn't so bad. And if I was being honest with myself, nothing had gone like I'd imagined it would.

We headed out, hand-in-hand. Main Street was paved with bricks, and the sidewalk was, too. The buildings were smashed together, the library next to the post office, and a little bakery beside that. Okay, Ashwood wasn't only not so bad, it was charming. And I found myself daydreaming about walking Evie to the library after school, and picking up cookies for a treat to go with dinner. It was the craziest thing, because at the center of the fantasy was a man I'd thought I hated—Jett Greyson.

Sure, I *had* hated him, but only because I hadn't really known him. Now, I was starting to, and I liked everything I saw. Every single inch...

Evie pulled my hand and plastered herself to the bakery window. "Look!"

There were cakes in the window, giant towers of frosting, one with ombre pink to blue, and one with a shiny purple and black swirl finish that looked like the photographs that satellites took of space.

"It's a unicorn cake! Do you see it? Do you see it?" Evie tapped on the glass, pointing at the ombre tower of sugar. I could see why she'd think it was unicorn-esque, with the colors and the sparkle on the white piped icing at the top.

"I see it."

"I *need* that cake."

"*Need* is a bit strong of a word for cake."

"Please?"

Her arms were full already, with the book and the stuffed unicorn. I was torn. It was difficult to say no, especially knowing how hard it had to be for her having her whole life thrown upside down. I wanted to make her happy, but I also didn't want her to think she could get whatever she wanted just by shoving out that pouty lip.

"You did do a good job on your lunch…" We'd eaten at a local diner. I'd had a veggie burger the size of my head, and she'd had a grilled cheese with a side of carrots. But she'd complained about the carrots with every bite—choking, gagging sounds, grabbing her throat and collapsing to the bench like it was killing her. In fact, she'd said a number of times that *I* was killing her. It earned us some odd looks, but I was vindicated when that last carrot left the plate. Into her stomach, not on the floor. I checked.

"I know. I ate *all* the carrots, even though they were gross." She made a sour face at the memory. "And I've been really good. Pleeeeeease."

Hands clasped, she gave me those big blue doe eyes, that perfectly-practiced pouty lip.

"Maybe."

"Yes!" She danced in victory.

"I didn't say yes. I said maybe."

"Yes, yes, yes." She twirled in a circle, and then grabbed the door handle and pulled. The door didn't budge. I put my hand above hers, and we pulled together.

The door opened, and the scent that greeted us…wow, what a scent. There was sugar, and spice, and yeast, and sugar. And more sugar. Did I mention sugar?

I took out my phone and snapped a few pics of some of the tasty treats, and one of Evie pushing her face on one of the glass cases. She was doing exactly what I wanted to do in this place, ogle and drool. After the pic, I reminded her not to touch the glass, but it was a great pic.

I wasn't sure that these snaps would make for article content, but it was always better to get everything I could instead of regretting not having them later. The bakery wasn't love, but chocolate definitely fit under the category of happiness. And if I couldn't use them for work, that weird glass face was a keeper.

"Can I help you?" A short woman with a ball of white hair and a pleasant smile met us at the counter.

"We're still—"

"That one." Evie pointed to a tray of frosted cookies. No surprise, they were decorated with winking unicorns.

"We'll take three of the unicorn cookies, please," I said.

"Yes!" Evie squealed in delight.

The woman behind the counter laughed and looked at her the way people always did when an adorable child was being cute instead of throwing a tantrum. She packed three cookies into a box and I paid before we headed back out into the heat.

Outside, I checked my phone. It was already six-thirty, and still no word from Jett. He'd call soon. He'd said he'd be back before dinner.

"Can I have my cookie?"

"After dinner."

Evie stuck out her lip. Again.

"Nope, not this time," I said. "I'm not falling for it."

Her eyes glossed over and her cheeks turned pink. Was she going to fake a cry?

I shook my head. "No way. *After dinner.*"

"Okay." She dropped her shoulders. "Is it time for dinner now?"

"Not quite. We're waiting on Jett."

"Are you going to eat with us?"

Surprised by the question, I shook my head. "No, just you and him."

"Oh." Evie took my hand and gave me a small smile. Was she disappointed?

"It's just going to be you and him," I said. "But we'll hang out again another time, I'm sure."

"Okay."

We started walking, heading back toward the bed and breakfast. Evie looked up at me, seeming to consider her words. "I thought you got three cookies so there'd be one for each of us."

"I did." I'd done it without thinking.

"You're not going to eat yours before dinner and make me wait until after, are you?"

"Of course not."

She nodded, seemingly appeased.

A block over, we were getting close to the playground where Evie had played in the morning. Her eyes were glued to the kids going down the slide.

"Hey, Aunt Paige?"

"Yeah?"

"Do you think if there's time before Jett gets back that maybe I can play some more?"

"Sure, I don't see why not."

"Thank you!" She handed me her book and plushie, and ran for the slide.

I took a seat on one of the empty benches and watched Evie play. It was the strangest thing. I felt like a phony, stepping into someone else's perfect life, what was supposed to be Marla's life. Maybe that wasn't fair. Marla hadn't been Jett's mate. They'd shared a night together, and from that night, a wonderful little person was born. But he hadn't loved her, and she hadn't known him well enough to really love him. I should have seen the red flags when I'd met him, or even before that—Marla never even knew he was a shifter. I hadn't told her about Evie, either. It was always something I figured we'd talk about later, sometime before Evie's first shift.

The afternoon sky faded to evening, the sun setting in the distance. The other kids went home, and the only people that remained at the park were me and Evie.

I pulled out my phone and dialed. It wasn't too much to expect that Jett would at least call by now, say he's running late. Or *something.*

It rang, and rang, and went to voicemail.

I hung up, and waited a little longer before calling for Evie.

Reluctantly, she walked back with me to the bed and breakfast, with minimal grumbling about how there was still a little light left and she could see just fine. Once we made it to my room, I grabbed a washcloth and scrubbed the dirt off of her face. That, too, came with some grumbling.

Faced with the mop of straw on her head, I was really tempted to pull out my brush, but after the washcloth, I decided not to push my luck. I didn't need Alethea—kudos to myself on remembering her name—from the front desk to call the police when Evie started screaming about how I was killing her. Like with the carrots.

Evie settled in on the bed and opened her book before giving me a pained look.

"I'm starving." Her stomach howled, agreeing with her.

I checked the time. It was already almost eight. "Let's order in."

"Pizza?"

I'd hoped to get something healthy into her, but at this point we were pushing bedtime and I didn't know if we could actually get something healthy delivered.

"I'll see what's around."

I checked my phone for local restaurants, and the only thing that delivered was a pizza place. Lucky kid. "All right, we'll get pizza."

"Yes!"

"But we're getting veggies on it."

"Noooooo." Evie melted onto the bed. "What's the point of pizza if you ruin it with carrots?"

"Not carrots this time," I said. "Spinach and peppers, maybe some mushrooms."

"Gross."

"You have to eat your pizza or you can't have your cookie." As soon as the words left my mouth, I realized how bad it sounded. It was just one night. Jett would be here soon, and I could tell him how pissed I was that he didn't call. One night of pizza, and the next time we'd eat something actually healthy. And I'd brush her hair.

While we waited for the food to arrive, Evie read her book, and I paced.

Had Jett decided he didn't have what it took to be a father? Was he as terrible of a person as I'd originally thought? Ditching his daughter because it was easy? No. More likely he got caught in his meeting longer than expected, and he was just terrible at being considerate.

I called again, this time from the bathroom so Evie wouldn't hear. Again, Jett didn't answer.

"Hey, asshole. It's really messed up for you to not call. This is not how parenting works. Get it together...Call me."

I hung up and realized I hadn't even said who I was. He'd figure it out.

I paced some more, until the doorbell rang. I realized my fists were balled, and I didn't want Evie to feel stuck in the middle of this, so I plastered on a fake smile and went out to pay for the pizza.

I settled in next to Evie on the bed, the big box between us.

"Hey, Aunt Paige."

"Yeah?" I handed her a piece.

"Do you think it would be okay if I called him 'Dad?'" She

searched my face, and I had to work harder to keep that smile plastered on. She deserved better than an asshole who didn't show up.

"Of course," I said. "If it makes you happy, you should."

"Yeah," she nodded. "I think I'd like that." She smiled at me then took a bite of her pizza. Her face contorted, but she didn't spit it out. "It's not as bad as I thought."

I laughed, and the smile I gave her was genuine.

CHAPTER TEN

JETT

*B*reath held, I lay still. Tall grass swished above me, with any luck, hiding my position. Darkness had fallen some time ago, and I'd lost track of which direction I was heading. *Away.* That was all that mattered.

Every so often, I'd hear voices, but never the words spoken. I tried to focus, but the pain in my chest and the drumming pulse in my ears dominated my senses. The more time that passed, the more my body mended, but I needed a place to rest to heal enough to make the trek home, and I was still too close to the Greenville wolves to breathe easy.

I stretched my paw and cringed at the stab in my side. Just a little farther and I could pause again. But for now, I had to keep moving.

I crept, keeping my belly to the dirt, and I checked the air for the scent of wolves. There was nothing. Blood, sure, but that was mine.

A few more feet and my legs gave out. I couldn't move another inch.

I fell to my side, my head spinning, and I looked up to the

stars above. They were a blurred mess of dancing shapes. My eyes burned, the lids impossibly heavy, until everything I had was gone and I couldn't fight anymore.

* * *

MY FACE WAS WARM, my body sore. I tried to roll over, and found it wasn't so easy. I peeked through still tired eyes only to realize I wasn't a man, but a wolf. How had I forgotten?

I stretched slowly, testing my limbs and my torso for injury. It wasn't agonizing. I wasn't one hundred percent, but I could make it home...once I figured out which way that was.

I rose to my feet and found myself in an unfamiliar field. That didn't tell me anything. But the recently risen sun would. I used its position to estimate which direction was which, and guessed that I was somewhere south and/or west of Greenville City, based on the position of the mountains in the distance.

Heading northeast, I found my feet much steadier than they'd been the night before. Too much time had passed. I had to get home. I had to warn Hawke.

I ran and I ran, until the scenery became familiar. After a few adjustments to my heading, I found myself in Butchers' territory. Careful not to be seen by any humans who happened to be out, I circled town and snuck over to the clubhouse lot.

I trotted over to the door before realizing I'd have to shift to open it. That was not ideal in full morning light, even though the lot butted up against the edge of the forest.

A familiar scent caught my attention before I had a chance to thoroughly scan for onlookers.

"Where the hell's my truck?"

86

I turned and found Brick trudging over to me. He opened the door, and I shifted as soon as I was safely inside.

"So?" Brick crossed his arms.

"It's a long story. Let me grab some pants and I'll tell you all about it. Get Hawke. He's going to want to hear this."

Brick narrowed his eyes and nodded. "Boardroom in five."

"Yeah." I jogged past the bar, where Shaundra watched me with a look of amusement and interest. Thankfully she didn't try to strike up conversation as I headed up to my room.

There, at the head of my bed was a pink backpack—Evie. It wasn't just war I had to worry about. I hadn't made it back to Paige's place last night. I hadn't even called.

It didn't matter that I had a damned good excuse. I'd fucked up, and they deserved better than that.

I'd apologize, and hope it would be enough. I could explain, but not until I'd talked to Hawke.

My mate and my daughter might hate me, but they were safe. The pack wasn't.

I threw on some clothes and headed back down to the business side of the building. I could sense Hawke and Brick were already inside the boardroom waiting for me.

Hawke was at the head of the table, his fingers steepled together as he watched me enter. Brick sat beside him, his face and posture stiff as stone.

I took a seat across from Brick.

"What the hell happened?" Hawke was cutting right to it.

"I never made it to Briggs," I said. "Security drugged me in the elevator, threw me in a trunk, and drove me to the middle of nowhere."

"Fuck." Brick slammed his fist against the table. "Now they know we're coming. We should have ambushed those bastards when we had the chance."

He wasn't wrong.

87

"Now there's no way we're getting close to Briggs," Brick said between gritted teeth. "Not without a whole lot of fire-power, storming the shit out of that fucking tower."

Hawke raised a hand, his gaze never leaving me. "Do they know who we are?"

"Possibly," I said.

"I can't believe this shit." Brick stood, knocking his chair to the ground.

"Sit." One word from Hawke, and Brick obeyed. The vein in his neck pulsed, and his face was red, his anger barely contained.

I turned to Hawke. "I gave them my card."

Brick grumbled but didn't say a word.

"No mention as to who I was representing," I said. "Only that I needed to talk with Briggs about what went down between their pack and the Silent Butchers."

Hawke leaned back in his chair. "It could be worse."

It could. They could have known what chapter I was from, and where to find us. All they had was my name and my phone number. It wasn't like I was in the phone book.

"As it stands, Briggs doesn't necessarily know anything about us. The next step—"

"One more thing," I said. I felt like an ass for having to admit this. Brick was right, I'd fucked up. "My phone was in my suit."

"Which is now in the Greenville pack's possession?" Hawke raised a brow.

I nodded. "Along with Brick's keys."

"Mother fucking...I can't believe I let you borrow my fucking truck."

"It's not parked in their lot," I said. "They won't find it right away, if they look for it at all."

"We can use this to our advantage." Hawke rose from his seat.

We both turned to him. Brick had to be thinking the same thing I was...how the fuck could he spin this shitshow from a burden into a boon? Not that it was a surprise—twisting reality was one of Hawke's specialties.

"You have the locator app turned on, Jett?"

"Yeah."

"Good. We're going to track your assailant. See if we can pinpoint a weakness," Hawke said.

Brick's eyes lit up. "We're going to war? Finally going to give these assholes the beating they deserve?"

"I can't see any other way forward." Hawke looked to me, as if waiting for answers.

I wished I had something to offer.

Hawke turned to Brick and nodded. "Looks like war."

Shit.

"Jett, bring me your laptop. Brick, where's that prospect?"

"I sent him on a beer run."

"The bar needs more kegs already?"

Brick smiled.

"All right," Hawke said. "As soon as he's back, bring him to me."

"Done." Brick nodded, and left the room.

Tracking my phone and figuring out if there was any useful data was a perfect job for Ray, the prospect. That kid was fantastic at programming. He'd had a job in Silicon Valley at twelve, then after he turned eighteen, he gave it all up to follow his dream to join the ranks of the Silent Butchers. There was a draw to this life, something special about riding with your brothers, and being a part of something bigger. It was similar to being a shifter with a pack, but in this brotherhood, our bonds were deeper. I wouldn't give them up for the world...or at least I'd never considered it until Paige.

Now I questioned everything about my life as it stood.

Maybe it was too much to expect to have a family of my own *and* the Butchers. The pain of that thought lingered like a frog in my throat, an ache in my chest.

I rose from my seat and headed for the door. I needed to get this done so I could return to Paige and Evelyn.

"Jett." I turned, and met Hawke's gaze. "If we can avoid bloodshed, we will."

I nodded and headed for the stairs.

But something drew me toward the bar...a feeling that I couldn't quite explain.

And when the door opened, I knew why.

Standing in the threshold was my mate, and holding her hand was my daughter. Evie looked absolutely delighted and waved at me, until she looked up at Paige. Then her smile slid into a frown.

Paige's eyes were red. She looked me over, and her expression hardened. "I'm glad you're fu—freaking alive."

"Paige—" I needed to fix this. I needed to say something.

She balled her fists and sucked in a deep breath, waiting for me to explain.

I didn't. I couldn't find the words. "I'm sorry."

"I don't know what you've been doing. You know what? I don't care. It doesn't matter. When you have a kid, you don't get to *not show up*."

One of the bike bunnies came out from the hall, in nothing but a thin tank top and a thong.

Paige's eyes went wide. "This is no life for Evie."

She turned and walked out the door, pulling Evelyn with her.

But Evelyn stared back at me, her arm outstretched. "Dad?"

She called me Dad. I opened my mouth and snapped it shut. What was I supposed to say? I had to say something.

My voice was brittle when the words came out. "I'm sorry, Evelyn."

My heart broke into a thousand pieces, and I didn't do a fucking thing. Not because I didn't want to, not because I didn't want them, but because Paige was right.

CHAPTER ELEVEN

PAIGE

*M*y eyes stung with unshed tears. I held them back and bit my tongue, determined to be strong.

Jett Greyson wasn't worth it. Not if this was how he treated us. Fate was a fucking bitch.

This man was not my mate, no matter what my heart told me. He didn't care about me, he didn't care about either of us. He'd spent his night fucking someone else while I took care of his kid. That's what I was to him—*the babysitter.*

I ran to my car, as fast as I could get Evie to run without knocking her down. I opened the back door for her and then climbed into the driver's seat. The car was a barrier, a wall between me and the world, between me and Jett.

With my fists clenched on the wheel, I mustered the courage to look back to the door. I expected him to follow, to try and explain his way out of this mess. He didn't.

He hadn't even bothered to try. Part of me was glad that the confrontation was over, and I didn't have to talk about it or listen to excuses. But as I sat here, I couldn't believe he wasn't going to try. That felt just as messed up, if not more so, than everything else.

Here was my article—*Love Hurts.* That was a song, though, right? How about *Love is a Rusty Blade Puncturing Your Heart.* It had a nice to ring to it. Ha.

"Aunt Paige?" Evie's soft voice pulled me from my bitter reverie. I tilted the rearview and met her gaze in the mirror, trying my damnedest to plaster on a smile.

"Yeah?"

"Are you okay?"

"Of course, sweetie. We're just changing plans is all." Better not to stay any longer in the parking lot or I was just as likely to go back inside and start yelling as I was to drive away.

I sucked in a deep breath and started driving. Where exactly we were headed...I had no idea. I couldn't go sit in my room. I needed distraction.

"Aunt Paige?"

"Yes?"

"Did I do something wrong?"

I swallowed hard and tried my damnedest to maintain my composure. "Of course not, Evie. Why would you think that?"

"You said I was going to be with...my dad."

My heart broke even more for her than it did for me. After everything Evie had been through, she assumed somehow she could be to blame when something went wrong.

"You'll see him soon," I said, not knowing if that was true or not. "But first we need to go to the store."

"What store?"

Good question. "Well, how much did your Aunt Sylvia pack for you when she dropped you off?"

"I packed myself." There was pride in her words instead of sadness. Good.

"Awesome," I said. "What did you pack?"

"My favorite pajamas."

"What else?"

"This shirt and pants."

"Great. Anything else?"

"My backpack?"

Not so great. But, that gave us something to do. Focus on the positive.

"Sounds like you need some clothes."

"But I *have* clothes."

"Not much with you, though you did do a great job packing."

"Oh." She sank in her seat. "I should have brought more."

"No. Aunt Sylvia should have brought more." Sylvia shouldn't have brought her here at all. She should have called me.

"Are you mad at her?"

"A little."

"I didn't want to leave."

"I know." It was an impossible situation. I parked the car in front of the only department store in town and turned around in my seat. "Maybe we should try to call your grandma and see how she's doing. What do you think?"

"Yes!"

After a few calls, I tracked down the nursing home Linda was staying in for her physical therapy. While I was getting connected to her room, Evie was doing flips in the back seat.

"Hello." Linda's voice was hoarse.

She didn't sound like herself at all, so much so that I wasn't sure they'd connected me to the right room. "Linda?"

"Who's this?"

"Paige."

"Oh, hi, dear. How are you?"

"I'm hanging in there. How are *you?*"

"The doctors never have anything good to say. It looks like I'm going to be stuck here for a while, and the food's terrible. But I'd love to hear about Evelyn. Sylvia told me she sent her to her father, and that you were going to visit. How is she?"

"She's standing on her head with her tongue out, right now. Do you want to talk to—"

Evie snatched the phone before I could finish my sentence.

"Grandma! I miss you."

"I miss you, too." Linda replied. "I hope I get to see you, and your new home sometime soon. Is it nice? Aunt Sylvia said it was nice."

Evie looked at me, her eyes wide. She shook her head, not knowing what to say. Then she looked down at the floor and squinched up her face. "I'm not coming home when you get back?"

"I wish you could. Can I talk to your Aunt Paige?"

Evie handed me the phone. The excitement she'd mustered had faded once again.

"I'm here."

"If it's not the life Sylvia said it was, I need you to look out for that girl. I can't do it anymore. I might not ever get out of here. Promise me you'll look after her."

Evie was staring out the window, with glassy eyes and a quivering lip.

"I promise." My chest was tight, but I kept my voice even.

"Be patient with her," Linda said. "Sometimes she makes bad choices. Sometimes it seems like she's misbehaving just for the sake of causing trouble. But if you give her time to reflect, keep your cool, and talk to her about what she's feeling, you'll see through to the vulnerable person who just wants to be loved."

It was great advice that could be applied to not just Evie, but her father, too. "I will. I promise. Linda, can I ask you something?"

"Anything."

It had been driving me crazy that Marla had told me she'd talked to Jett about the pregnancy, so I had to ask. "Did Marla tell you about coming to Ashwood when she found out she was pregnant?"

"Oh. You mean about talking to Jett."

"Yes."

"She was too embarrassed to tell you. She saw him with another woman and fled. She never told him about Evie."

How had I not known? I tried to remember. Marla had told me she was going to tell him. And when she came home she said it was over. She said she'd seen him. She'd given short answers, and I'd let it go. She'd led me to believe she'd told him, but I guess she'd never said the words. I wished I could tell her that it was okay. She never needed to lie to me, or to pretend anything. I loved her. But in learning the truth, a weight lifted.

"Thanks for telling me. Take care, Linda."

"You, too, dear."

I hung up and climbed out of the car. It was up to me to make sure Evie was cared for. We could return to my apartment in Murrayville. Maybe that was the best move, but even if it was easier, I couldn't go back. Not yet. Not with the way I left things with Jett. He had an explanation...didn't he? At the very least, he should have some say of what happened to his daughter. More than that, I didn't want to give up on a man I *knew* was my mate, even if that made me a fool.

I opened Evie's door for her. She slid out slowly, her whole body sagging as she dragged her feet. I walked slowly to accommodate the intense moping. I felt a bit like that on the inside, myself. But with Evie, everything was right there on the surface.

Once inside the store, I grabbed a cart. "Want to ride?"

She looked up at me, and I could see a spark there, pushing back against the crappy hand life had thrown at her. She nodded.

She climbed up between me and the handle. I reached around her and pushed.

"I'm thinking we need to start in the candy aisle." I couldn't see her face, but I looked down anyway.

"Candy?" I could hear the smile in her voice.

"Oh yeah. I need some chocolate big time."

"Me, too!"

In the candy aisle, I grabbed a big bar of one of my favorites, caramel and peanut butter stuffed. Evie grabbed an arm-full of boxes and bags. Her little eyes sparkled, and she smiled at me. "Please?"

"Throw it in. We're doing girls' day right."

"Yes! Thank you, Auntie Paige. You're the best!"

If only taking care of a kid was always that easy. Hell, not just a kid, but life in general.

"Hop on," I said. "Time for clothes."

Evie did as I said, and I pushed the cart. There were racks and racks of kids' stuff, and I had no idea what to pick, let alone what size she wore. Thankfully, Evie knew exactly what she liked. She ran over to a shirt with a sunglass-clad racoon on it.

"It's perfect!" She pulled on the shirt, struggling to get the hanger from the rack.

"It really is," I said. "Do you know what size you need?"

She shook her head.

"Let's check." I looked at the back of her collar. 6/7. The shirts on the rack only had a single size, not two put together. The sleeves of the shirt she had on were about two inches too short, so I guessed we should go a size up. "I'm going to say 8."

"Just like how old I almost am."

"Yes, it is." I guessed that's how kids' sizes worked. I had a lot to learn, but we were doing it, figuring it out, one racoon shirt at a time.

She ran around, weaving between the racks and hiding up inside a few of them, giggling when I pretended not to know where she was. After the third time in the same shirt rack, Evie popped her head out before I 'found' her.

"Hey, Aunt Paige."

"Aww, I found you!"

"No. That doesn't count. It only counts if I don't come out first."

"I don't know. Seems like it should count to me." I crossed my arms in mock sternness.

Evie shook her head. "I was just thinking. You said cake isn't something you *need.*"

"That's true."

"But you also said you needed chocolate. Those are both treats."

I shrugged. "True, true. You caught me. But, sometimes needs change."

"I'm going to remember that next time we go to the bakery."

I laughed. "I'm sure you will."

Evie picked a few more shirts, and some stretchy pants— because she had great taste and comfy pants were the best pants. I insisted on underwear and socks, because like an animal, Evie seemed perfectly content without.

After clothes, we hit the groceries. There wasn't much to choose from, but I figured we needed something healthier than pizza to eat. And the chocolate wasn't going to cut it.

The bed and breakfast provided meals with the cost, if we were there on time, but not snacks, so I picked up some mixed veggies and nuts. Evie picked apple slices.

After the store, we washed clothes at the laundromat, played at the park, and ate. The entire day I waited for Jett to call, but he didn't. By the time night rolled around, we were back in the bed and breakfast, and I had decided on a plan. We'd give him one more day to man up before we left for the city.

A soft whimpering came from the bathroom. I rose from my bed and listened by the door. She was crying.

I knocked. "Evie, are you okay?"

She sniffled and opened the door.

Her hair was soaking wet as she stood there in one of her new sets of jammies, staring at the floor. Tears streamed down her face, and she sniffled once again.

I knelt down in front of her and put my hands on her shoulders. "What's wrong?"

"Aunt Paige? How come no one wants me?"

My heart shattered and I pulled her into my arms.

"Sometimes life throws us one curveball after another, until there's a whole pile of balls crushing us. But just because they can't be with you right now doesn't mean they don't want to. Okay?"

She nodded slowly.

I squeezed her again. "And guess what else?"

"What?" She rubbed the back of her hand across her face, smearing tears and snot all over the place.

"*I* want you. And I'm not going anywhere without you."

CHAPTER TWELVE

JETT

*M*y eyes stung and my muscles were sore. I was feeling the toll of the past few days, and of staying up all night. With Brick heading up surveillance on the Greenville City Pack, I was free to attend to my personal business. I could have gone after Paige the day before. I could have called her, or stopped by, or tried to reach out. But I hadn't. I wasn't ready. But I had something to show her now, something better than words.

With Evie's pink backpack strapped to my back, I drove my bike to the bed and breakfast. After I rounded the last turn, I noticed Paige's car parked in front of the building with the trunk open. I slowed to a stop, and found Evie waving from the back seat at me. I waved back and smiled.

The trunk closed, and there was Paige.

The look she gave me reaffirmed what I already knew— she was pissed. At me. And I knew I deserved it.

"Where are you two headed?" I asked.

"Really?" She crossed her arms. "You come by and talk to me like you have a right to know what we're doing, or where we're going. Like everything is fucking fine? Because it's not."

I deserved that. "I know. And I'm sorry."

"Sorry for which part? For acting like an asshole, or for getting caught?"

The accusation stung, but also confused me. What did she think I'd been caught doing? "Give me a chance to explain."

"Go ahead. We're talking right now. Lay it on me." Her eyes narrowed and she shifted her stance.

I needed to choose my words carefully. I'd hurt her and I didn't want to make things worse. I pulled up to the curb, parked, and climbed off my bike.

Sweet with bite—her scent struck me like a bat to the chest. Between all the other shit going on in my life, I'd hardly given time to the woman who was my future. That was going to change. Everything was about to change.

"I'd like to show you something."

She sucked in a deep breath and let her arms drop back to her sides. "Show me what?"

"It's just a short drive."

She frowned and turned her attention to the back seat of her car.

"We'll give you an hour. Then we're going home."

She was really going to leave. After yesterday, I couldn't blame her for being hurt, or blame her for running.

"I can work with an hour."

She looked me over, and her face hardened once again. "Where's your truck?"

"It's a long story."

Her back went stiff and her eyes narrowed. "Of course it is."

"I'll tell you everything. I swear."

She considered me, and my heart beat a little faster as I waited for her to decide. Just one hour. All I needed was a chance to explain, a chance to show her. After she knew the truth, well, I wasn't sure what she'd decide.

"Fine. I'll drive."

We climbed into the car, and two sticky little hands covered my eyes.

"Guess who." Evelyn attempted to lower her voice as she spoke, giving her usual softness a gruff tone.

I reached up and patted my hands over hers. "Hmmm," I said. "Is it Paige?"

She laughed and let go. "Are you coming back to Murrayville with us?"

The reminder that they were leaving hurt. "We're going on an adventure."

"To the park?"

"Better. But it's a secret until we get there."

She leaned her head over my shoulder and whispered, "Is it ice cream?"

"No," I said. "But that's fun, too."

Paige tapped Evelyn's shoulder. "Strap in. It's time to go."

Evelyn did as she was told, and I looked over at Paige beside me. She had her hands on the wheel, ready to go.

"Where to?"

"Follow this street to the end and take a right." I didn't take my eyes off her, and if it bothered her, she didn't show it.

The seatbelt flattened her loose shirt over her chest, highlighting the swell of her ample breasts. She really was gorgeous, from her thick eyelashes and full lips to the feminine curve of her thighs. I could look at her all day and all night and never lose this sense of awe.

"A left up ahead." We were reaching the edge of town. It wouldn't be long before we were there.

"That's...a dirt road." Paige glanced over at me.

"Oh, I know where we are!" Evelyn kicked the back of my seat and tapped on the window.

"Shhh," I said. "Don't spoil the surprise."

We turned down the dirt road and followed the trees to where the forest was thick.

"You two have been out here?" Paige asked.

Evelyn just kicked the seat and said nothing.

"Veer to the right when the road splits," I said.

"Okay."

The trees broke to the field of grass I'd cut the night before, to the cabin that I hoped could be our home someday.

"Where are we?" Paige turned to me, and the tension she'd shown before the drive had faded.

I might actually have a shot at this.

"Home," I said.

"Can I get out?" Evelyn already had her seatbelt off and was standing between us.

"Sure." I nodded. "Just stay in the front yard."

She hopped out of the car and ran around in the field with her arms spread wide. Paige made no move to climb out, so I didn't either. This could be our chance to talk, for me to tell her everything without Evelyn overhearing.

"What do you mean, *home*?" There was vulnerability in Paige's soft expression. She wanted this to work as much as I did, or at least that's how I chose to read her.

"This is the cabin I grew up in. It's mine. And it can be *ours*."

Paige huffed. "You're unbelievable." Her tone suggested this was not a compliment. "You talk about *our* house like there's an *us*."

"I want there to be. Don't tell me that you don't feel the pull. We're mates."

"I refuse to accept that my mate would abandon me and his kid while he's fucking some—"

"Wait." What the hell was she talking about?"

"Wait, what? And by the way, your hour is already a third of the way over."

"Paige." I touched her hand and I felt it, a jolt of electricity spreading from such a simple contact. Her lips parted, ever so slightly, and she didn't pull away. "Paige, I haven't even looked at another woman since I met you."

"What?"

"I only want you."

"That woman at the bar…"

"Not mine."

She flattened her lips into a line and watched Evelyn rolling in the grass. Was it that hard to look me in the eye?

"Then where were you?" She turned, and her big chestnut eyes were glazed with unshed tears. "Why didn't you show up when you said? Why didn't you answer your phone or call me back?"

"I want you to know that it won't last."

"What won't last?"

"The threat."

She pulled her hand back. "What threat?"

"There's another pack, not too far from here. Greenville. They hired another chapter of the Silent Butchers, then betrayed them, turned them in to the Tribunal for the job Greenville hired them to do."

"That doesn't make any sense."

"I know. That's why I went for a peaceful meeting, to hear their side of the story."

"That's the meeting you asked me to watch Evie for."

"Yeah."

"So what went wrong?"

"I probably should have seen it coming." What should I say? What should I hold back? I didn't want to scare her. "They attacked me. I was lucky to escape with my life."

She squeezed my hand.

"I lost my phone."

"And your truck?"

"Well, the truck belongs to my friend, Brick, but yes, I lost his keys, too."

"And that's why you didn't come for Evie." Paige looked back to Evie, who was rolling in the grass.

"Yes. It took me until morning to get home."

Paige looked back at me. "Are you okay?"

"I am now."

Evie ran over to the hood of the car and waved at us. Paige waved back.

"So they're still out there...wanting to hurt you."

"Yes."

"So come away with us. Back to Murrayville."

She couldn't know how much it meant that she wanted me to be with them. "I wish I could."

"You mean you don't want to." Her voice was soft, her tone bitter. But she didn't let go of my hand.

"No," I said. "I mean, I can't leave my pack. Not now, not like this. They're the only family I've ever known, and they need me."

"We—Evie needs you, too."

"What do you have in Murrayville?" I asked.

"An apartment, a job."

"What do you do?" I couldn't believe I didn't already know.

"I'm a writer."

"Do you have to be in the city for your job?"

She stared into my eyes, and I knew the answer. She was afraid.

"No."

"Let me show you something." I opened the door and climbed out. Paige did the same. "Down that way, there's a treehouse Hawke and I built when we were kids. It's still in pretty good condition. And over there...do you hear that?"

"A stream."

I nodded.

"And this cabin...well, it needs a lot of work." I took a risk and captured her hand. She was warm and soft, and a perfect fit.

Evelyn grabbed my other hand, and the three of us walked up to the door.

"I want to go inside!" Evelyn said.

"Me, too." Paige smiled down at her.

At the door, a pang of nerves hit me. Everything was going so well, what happened if Paige didn't like it? What happened if I fucked this up?

I turned the knob. "Remember, it needs a lot of work."

Evie raced in and ran down the hall. "Which bedroom is mine? Ooh, I want the big one."

There was the sound of squeaking springs.

"No jumping on the bed," Paige yelled. Then she looked at me. "There is a bed to make that sound, right?"

"There is."

I'd pulled out the old generator for light, grabbed gloves and trashbags from the shed, cut the grass, and vacuumed up all the glass the night before. I'd tried to make sure everything was safe, and as clean as I could make it in a short time. If Paige said yes, I'd do more. I'd renovate everything. Paint the walls, tear out the flooring, remodel the kitchen. Everything was dated, and even if it wasn't...I didn't want it to look anything like the house I'd grown up in. It could be built from the same bones, but this time, it would be a real home.

"It's..." Paige looked around.

"I know," I said. "Musty, shitty. But it won't stay that way. I'm going to tear everything out."

Paige shot me a questioning look. "I was going to say charming."

CHAPTER THIRTEEN

PAIGE

*J*ett slid his hands into his pockets and shifted his gaze. I could swear there was something off, maybe what I said, though I had no idea what was wrong with complimenting his house. He'd brought me here to show it to me. It was polite to say something nice. And really it was more than charming. It was a cabin full of potential.

Let's say we actually did the whole mating, baby making, family thing. What better place to raise a bunch of shifter kids than our own private forest? I didn't mind leaving the city. I could work anywhere I could get cable internet, but that wasn't what scared me.

I was afraid to jump all-in with a man I still knew almost nothing about. I was afraid of the dangerous life he led. He said the threat was almost over, but who was to say there wouldn't be another after that, and another? Constantly looking over my shoulder was no way to live.

"The kitchen's this way." He started walking, closing himself off.

A few moments ago, outside, he'd been holding my hand. I followed, wondering what had caused the change.

"Did your parents move away?" I asked.

"No." Jett stopped and flipped on the light in the kitchen. "They both died."

"I'm so sorry."

"Don't be." He turned around. "The cabinets will all need to be torn out, but I know a guy who does amazing custom work. Imagine stainless steel appliances, butcher block countertops."

I touched his shoulder, but he didn't turn around.

He pointed and said, "Maybe take out that wall over there."

"Jett?" I stepped up beside him.

"What about your family?" he asked. "Are they in Murrayville?"

He didn't want to talk about his parents. In the car, he'd said Hawke was his family. He cared for his pack, but not his kin. I wanted to ask more, but he made it clear he didn't want to talk about it. I couldn't get to know him if he didn't let me in, but I also had no right to demand he tell me everything the second the question popped into my head.

But what if they'd died because of the MC?

I wanted to ask, but if I expected him to answer my questions, I should answer his. Relationships took time and work, fated mates or not.

"No," I said. "My parents aren't in Murrayville. I didn't really fit in so well back home, so I ran off to the city for college, then settled there. It's just an okay apartment, but it's mine."

I left off the last thought, that I wasn't committed to staying in Murrayville. I didn't have any ties anymore, without Marla and Evie there. And I couldn't imagine going back without Evie. But I wasn't ready to admit any of that to Jett.

He took a step closer, and I breathed in his spiced cider scent. He brushed a hair from my cheek, leaving a pleasant warmth in the wake of his touch. "Instead of fitting in," he said, "I bet you stood out. Just as you do here in Ashwood, or like you would anywhere you went."

Swoon. A touch of sweetness, and I was ready to tear off my clothes and jump him. Okay, maybe I would have felt the urge even if he was a dick.

He *could* be a dick, but that was just his shell. Beneath that, I caught a glimpse of a man who was searching for his place in the world, trying hard to be a good person. For me. For Evie.

"You used to live in Murrayville, too, right?" It's where he'd met Marla, after all. And I still hadn't gotten the full story on that. She'd said he'd lied about becoming a lawyer.

"I went to law school there. Came back after I finished my degree."

So he was a lawyer. Lawyer and biker didn't seem like they went together, but people were complicated. Jett was complicated, and full of surprises.

"Ahhhhh!" The high-pitch squeal made my heart skip a beat.

Evie.

I raced down the hall, terrified that she'd fallen off the bed and broken her arm, or worse. I found her on the bedroom floor, with a huge grin. She hadn't cried out in agony, but in delight. In her arms was a stuffed animal.

"You scared me," I said, my voice shaking with the adrenaline of my race down the hall.

"Look what I found." She held out her treasure—it was a rhinoceros...with a mustache.

"You have good taste," Jett said from behind me. I turned

around and found him leaning on the doorframe with a crooked grin. "That's Mr. Stabbyface. I'm surprised he'd still around. I figured he was gone a long time ago."

"Stabby...face?" I gave Jett a disapproving glare.

He shrugged. "He has horns on his head."

"And a mustache." Evie's eyes sparkled and her grin was wider than I'd ever seen. "He was in a box in the closet. Can I have him?"

She was using her big blues to their fullest, batting her lashes like a pro. It was a smart alternative to the pouty lip.

I hoped Jett didn't have anything inappropriate stored in his room, since it seemed Evie was making herself right at home.

"Promise to take care of him?" Jett lifted a brow.

Evie nodded emphatically.

"Well, okay then," Jett said. "He's yours."

"Thanks, Dad!"

Jett flinched and his eyes widened, but only for a second. After that, he smiled. This was the second time she'd called him Dad, and apparently it was going to take him some time to get used to it.

"You're welcome, squirt." He turned to me and nodded toward the hall.

I followed him out, wondering if he wanted to talk more about kitchen cabinets, or about something that really mattered. He stopped in the living room, far enough away from Evie that she wouldn't hear us if we spoke softly.

Jett turned to me, trapping me in the deep pools of his blue eyes. They called to me like the ocean, beckoning me to jump into the waves. Everything else about him was hard— his ripped abs, his broad shoulders, the sharp lines of his bearded jaw. But in his eyes, I saw longing. I saw a search for more than life had offered. I saw me.

Butterflies fluttered in my stomach. My breathing quickened. Now that we were alone, I wanted to kiss him. My lips tingled at the thought of the sensation, and I bit my bottom lip to make it stop.

"Paige."

He took a step closer, his warm, masculine scent fogging my brain. I knew I should scold him about the stuffed animal name. He could have told her it was called Pokey or Steve, or anything other than Stabbyface. But instead, I nodded, my body ready to agree to anything, all reasonable thought completely forgotten. How could this man have such an effect on me?

"Paige, I want you to stay. Please. Stay in Ashwood, with me." His voice was deep and gravelly, doing dangerous things to my insides.

"I don't know." Like a badass, I resisted his charms, by which I mean, I didn't throw myself at him.

"Keep Evie with you until the Greenville issue blows over. Stay in town. I'm not asking you to promise me forever. I'm just asking for a chance."

"A chance." I wished I could have said I had to think about it. But at the very least, I didn't let the words tumble out of my mouth like a desperate teenager. I paused a half-second before saying, "I can do that."

* * *

I'D THOUGHT about arguing on the drive back. After we returned to the bed and breakfast, I was still thinking about all the reasons I should have said no. And when I went to bed, I continued to wrestle with my decision to stay.

Did I like him? Yep, even if I knew I shouldn't.

Did I want him? Hahaha, yeah, that shouldn't count as part of the equation.

Would I have enjoyed licking whipped cream off his washboard abs? Okay, really off topic.

Was it safe to stay? That's the part I wanted to ignore, but couldn't. Yes, it would be fantastic to get to know my mate, to actually give *us* a chance. *But* he was *attacked.* Not a long time ago, not in another life, when he was a different man. It *just* happened. What if I'd been with him? *What if Evie had been with him?*

These were the things I had to remember when he arrived this morning. These were the problems I couldn't forget when he touched my hand or when he said my name in that deep, gruff voice.

A knock at the door pulled me from my thoughts.

"I'll get it!" Evie ran over to the door and fiddled with the lock.

I went over to help her, hoping it was him.

Jett had said he'd be here before late morning to pick us up for more time at the cabin, time together. And it seemed like this time he was keeping his word.

A hint of his spiced scent greeted me as I approached the door, and my body responded with every nerve coming to life. It was like not eating for a week and then stepping into a bakery. And then images of whipped cream filled my head…

Evie opened the door. "I got it!"

There was Jett, but also someone else, a woman. A memory flashed through my head, one of a near-naked woman close to Jett in the clubhouse. A flare of anger pulsed through my veins. I looked between them, wondering who she was supposed to be, and attempting to suppress the urge to not so politely ask. I didn't need to be jealous. This wasn't the same woman, and if she had been, he'd said that she wasn't with him. Jett and I were *mates.* Or at least we were supposed to be.

"Hey." I was pretty pleased with how even my voice

sounded.

"Good morning." Jett looked down at Evie, who was happily dragging him in. "I brought a friend along today."

A friend. Totally not jealous. I forced my fists to relax.

"Shaundra, this is Paige." Jett gestured toward me.

Shaundra smiled. "Nice to meet you."

"You, too."

"And this is Evelyn." Jett lifted the hand that was firmly still stuck in Evie's grasp.

"Nice to officially meet you, Evelyn. I hear we're going to get to hang out today."

Oh. That was news to me.

Evie looked from me to Jett. He patted her shoulder. "Shaundra has two daughters."

"That's right," Shaundra nodded. "One of them is seven years old, too."

"That's just like me!" Evie grabbed her hand. "Does she like unicorns?"

"Unicorns?" Shaundra said. "Who *doesn't* like unicorns?"

Evie wiggled with excitement. And I had to admit, I liked this chick, too. I felt a little bad about my initial reaction to Jett bringing her along. I had been wrong. Shaundra was great.

"So what do you say, Evie? Ready to come hang out at my house?"

"Wait." Evie ran and grabbed her stuffed unicorn and then headed for the door. "Bye, Dad. Bye, Paige."

She didn't even turn to look back.

"I guess that's my cue." Shaundra laughed, and headed after her.

The door clicked shut, and the air changed—warmer, heavier. It was just me and Jett. *Alone.* We were finally going to have time to get to know each other, and not just stolen moments between parenting.

Jett took a step closer to me, and another. I held my breath, my heart fluttering in my chest. *Kiss me.* Silence seemed to go on forever, an eternity of him not touching me, of him not shoving his tongue down my throat. I had to say something. Anything.

"Shaundra seems nice." My voice came out more squeak than the cool, collected calm I'd hoped for.

"She is. But I don't want to talk about her. I want to talk about you. About us."

I nodded a little too emphatically.

"Are you hungry?" he asked.

Uh…that was not the talk I'd expected. "Sure."

"Have lunch with me."

"Sure."

His blue eyes flashed, and I knew this was it. He was going to kiss me, maybe do more. If I had my way, he'd do a lot more. Goosebumps prickled across the back of my neck as his fingers brushed mine.

He squeezed my hand in his. "Let's go."

It took my brain time to catch up to my feet. We were walking down the stairs, outside, to his motorcycle. I was already about to burst, throw him on the ground and tear off his clothes in the middle of the street. I couldn't imagine my lust-filled brain settling while I was pressed up against him with the bike vibrating beneath me.

It had to be the mating instinct. I'd never been so sex-crazed before. Once we sealed the deal, I'd return to normal functioning. As I pressed my chest against his back, wrapped my arms around him, and melted against him on the seat, I wasn't so sure I could ever be this close to him and *not* want to jump him. Maybe that wasn't such a bad thing.

The engine started and I squeezed him, burying my face in his leather jacket. Maybe this was what love was going to be like for us. I hoped it was.

CHAPTER FOURTEEN

⤜⤛

JETT

The wheels jostled and bumped as I slowed the bike on the rough dirt driveway. The trip over had been too short, and I didn't want Paige to pull away. But we had plenty of time, and I had plenty of ideas for how we could spend it.

I parked, and Paige lingered. Her fingers spread over my chest, and I only wished my shirt wasn't between her skin and mine. Slowly she pulled away, and I could still feel the warmth of her touch.

"We're eating in today, huh?" Her voice was soft behind me, and the bike rocked as she hopped off.

"Actually, I have something else in mind." I climbed off, and captured her hand before leading her to the door.

"Oh? It does *seem* like we're going inside."

"Only to grab something."

"Okay then." She followed me without question, and I hoped my nerves didn't show. I had no idea if this was the kind of thing she was going to like or not. We still didn't really know each other yet, but I wanted to know her. And I wanted her to know me.

I'd never cared what a woman thought of me. Well, maybe with the exception of Shaundra, but that was because she was like one of the guys. Respect of my pack meant everything to me, but now, I found Paige's approval meant more.

I led her to the kitchen and handed her the blanket I'd left folded on the counter. I grabbed the basket I'd packed the night before from the fridge. After we'd called it a day, I had returned to do a little more work around the house, and to prepare this lunch for Paige.

"A picnic basket?" she said. "All bears aren't Yogi, you know."

Had I offended her? My heart sank at the thought. "Does that mean you don't like picnics? We can do something—"

"No, no." She shook her hands at me and cringed. "Sorry, I'm just nervous. A picnic sounds lovely. Really."

"No pressure, no expectations, no need to worry." I kissed her temple and breathed her in. She was so damned sweet. I pulled away before I ended up pushing things she didn't want, that she wasn't ready for, which was difficult, because more than anything *I wanted her.*

A shade of deep rose tinted her cheeks and she nodded.

"Ready?" I asked.

"Yes."

I led her into the forest. The path wasn't as wide as I would have liked, but it would wear down with time as it had in the past. Paige had no trouble keeping up, and seemed completely at ease climbing over trunks and ducking under hanging branches.

"You're a natural out here." I looked back over my shoulder at her, and she smiled.

"I wasn't always a city girl."

She'd said before that she hadn't fit in at home. I wanted to ask more about it, but to be fair, I hadn't shared much about myself when she'd asked about my parents. Better to start with safe and generic, let her decide what she wanted to share.

"Do you come from a small town like this?" I asked.

"Pretty much," she said. "Frozen Peaks. It's almost entirely a bear community."

The prison I'd visited was in Frozen Peaks. I wondered if the little town I'd flown in from was her hometown.

"Have you heard of it?" Paige asked.

"Yes." Did she know about the prison there? What about that town made her feel she didn't belong? I wasn't sure what to ask, so I said nothing. We kept walking, the sounds of the stream growing louder as we approached.

"No." She stopped in her tracks.

"What?" I turned around, and found her brows furrowed as she stared me down. What had I done wrong?

"You said you want to get to know me, but every time we talk about who we are, or our pasts, you get all weird."

"I'm not..." I clenched my jaw, unsure of how to respond.

"I'll tell you what." A flash of something crossed her face. Mischief?

I looked at her, concerned about what would come next.

"We take turns asking questions. And if I ask you something, you tell me the whole truth even if it's uncomfortable."

I wasn't sure I wanted to promise that. It was a lot to ask. But, if I had the same opportunity in return... "And if I ask you a question, you respond honestly no matter what the question is."

She chewed on her lip, her cheeks flushed with color.

Holy fuck, that was sexy. I wanted to nibble her lip.

"Fair enough," she finally said. "I'm game if you are."

"I'm in." My voice came out dark, and with it the sweet scent of her desire met my nose. Part of this game might make me uncomfortable, but she was giving me free rein for some fun. I turned around and started walking. "We're almost there."

A little farther, and the trees broke to the stream. The water was shallower than I remembered it from when I was a boy. Maybe that was just because I was bigger.

Paige stepped up beside me and looked over the water. "This is really nice."

"I used to play here as a boy, with Hawke."

She nodded. "I bet it was a blast to splash around on hot summer days. Were you thinking of bringing Evie here?"

"Yes, once we all move into the cabin. My turn."

"What?" She blinked hard and straightened her back.

"It's my turn, remember."

"Okay, okay. The game was my idea, after all. So what's your...ask away." She bit her lip again, and it made my cock pulse.

"Tell me why you didn't like living in Frozen Peaks," I said.

"That is a command, not a question." She raised a brow and spread the blanket out by the bank. The scent of her desire fueled my own.

I set the basket down on the ground and helped smooth the fabric. "I think you like when I tell you what to do."

"That's not a question, either."

I sat down on the center of the blanket and tapped the ground beside me. "Sit with me."

She knelt down and crawled over, her big brown eyes intent on my mouth, and took a seat beside me.

"Are you going to ask me a question?" She inhaled deeply as she touched my fingers.

"Do you like it when I tell you what to do?"

"Yes." Her voice was soft and breathy.

I leaned closer, and she didn't pull away. This wasn't going anything like I'd planned, and I fucking loved it. I ran my hand slowly up her arm, and her heartbeat quickened. My cock ached for her, every moment together more difficult than the next. I needed her. She was mine.

"My turn." Paige cleared her throat. "What happened...with your parents?"

Instant turn-off.

But fair was fair.

"My parents fought a lot when I was a kid," I said. Talking about it, hell, just thinking about it, made me uncomfortable. But we agreed to the whole truth, and there was more to tell. "My dad was a drunk, treated my mother like shit. She became a vacant shell, and when she wasn't throwing things back at my father, she was ignoring that he hit me, too."

"I'm so sorry."

"She died first. Overdose of sleeping medication. Turns out he'd cared enough that he killed himself not long after. It was a mixed bag for me. It felt like shit losing them, but also, it was a bit of a relief." I'd never said that out loud before. It left me with a weird feeling. I didn't like it.

Paige looked down at the water and didn't say anything, then she rose to her feet and met my gaze with a ferocity I hadn't expected.

"You opened up," she said. "Thank you so much for that. Now it's my turn."

I watched her with interest, unsure what she meant.

"You want to know about my damage. I always hated being the big girl. Taller than the other shifter women in my town. Chubbier."

"Paige, you're not—"

She raised a hand. She had more to say. "I wasn't into any of those lumberjack types anyway, but it still hurt that no one ever wanted me."

I wanted her. There wasn't a damned thing I'd change

about her body. She was tall—I loved that. She had womanly curves—I loved that, too.

"I know that we're supposed to be forever, that we're supposed to fall in love. But I don't know what a guy like you would see in a woman like me. And I want to show you my damage."

She pulled her shirt up over her head and dropped it to the ground. Her breasts were big and beautiful, and still hidden in her bra.

I rose to my feet but gave her space. I wasn't going to cut her off again. This was what she wanted. She wanted to show herself to me. When she was ready, I'd show her the truth. She wasn't damaged, she was beautiful.

She toed off her shoes, slid down her pants. And she lifted her chin as gooseflesh crossed over her bare skin.

"This is me," she said. "And if you don't like what you see, well—"

I pulled her in to my chest, threaded my fist in her hair, and I kissed her like the world fucking depended on it. My tongue was claiming, igniting. Her breasts heaved softly as I held her close.

Her lips were supple and minty, and she moaned gently against my lips.

"Paige." I leaned my forehead against hers. "You aren't chubby or too tall. You're gorgeous, smart, caring, and absolutely fucking perfect."

She giggled and shook her head like she didn't believe it. But it was true. There was no one more perfect for me than her. And I couldn't understand how I was so lucky to have her as my mate.

"Are you going to ask me a question or should I go again?" she asked.

"You just asked me another question." I smiled against her lips and gave her a peck. I ran my palms over her back, reaching down to squeeze her ass. It was the perfect handful, and the noise she gifted me with when I pinched her —delicious.

"I guess you'll have to get two in a row." She smiled and pulled the jacket down off my shoulders.

"Okay," I said. "Paige, will you be my mate?"

"Yes. A thousand times, yes."

I kissed her deep, the wolf inside of me growling to mark her for the whole fucking world to know, my cock pressing hard against my fly to be inside of her *now*. I pulled back and cupped her breast in my palm, flicking my thumb over the thin fabric of her bra. Her nipple tightened into a bud and her eyes fluttered shut.

"Question number two..." I leaned in and scraped my teeth over the lobe of her ear. She whimpered and arched her back, pressing her breast harder into my hand. "How many times do you want to come?"

CHAPTER FIFTEEN

※

PAIGE

*M*y fingers fumbled as I tried to lift the hem of his shirt up over his head, to undo his pants. My body was fire, he was the kindling, and I fucking needed the log. I'd never felt so accepted by someone. I thought we were a terrible pairing from the start, but I was wrong. I was wrong about everything.

This was the love story I'd waited for my entire life, and none of it was happening like I'd expected. I'd thought I wanted roses and candle-lit dinners. Turned out, it could be a blanket in the middle of the woods, and I couldn't imagine anything more perfect. It was him, and it was us. This was what love was really like.

Jett helped me with his clothes, and didn't struggle at all with my bra. Sure, he'd probably unclasped a hundred of them, but the past didn't matter. We were the present, we were the future, and we were mates.

The cold air faded to the heat of his touch. He grazed his teeth across my jaw, down my neck, slow deliberate kisses with a tease of more. I wanted everything he would give me, wanted him to mark my flesh as his.

I grabbed hold of his shoulders as he sank to his knees, kissing down my chest. My breasts were heavy with need, my nipples tight buds begging to be taken by his warm mouth. He stilled my body with one hand on my hip, while he kneaded my breast with his other hand.

I closed my eyes and listened to the call of a bird in the distance, to the babbling flow of the stream beside us, and the world became distant as Jett flicked his tongue over my nipple. Heat pooled between my legs, zings of pleasure shooting from every touch, every lick.

"So fucking beautiful." His voice was rich with desire, and with restraint.

How long had he wanted this? Since we met, just like I had? Was foreplay as an exquisite a torture for him as it was for me? He seemed to be savoring me, taking his time, but what I really wanted was fast, rough. I wanted him inside me. Now.

He kissed lower, trailing down my stomach.

"This is...amazing." I gasped as he reached around and grabbed my ass.

He nipped just beside my bellybutton with his teeth, and I squealed in surprise.

"I love the little noises you make for me. I can't wait to see what else I can make you do."

Holy fuck. Yeah, at this rate I was going to explode from words and kisses alone.

"I want…"

He went lower, licking the inside of my thigh. I inhaled sharply as the cool air brushed against my wet skin. It wasn't just his tongue that was leaving me wet.

"I want to feel you inside of me." It wasn't the kind of thing I was used to saying, but with the way he talked to me...well, what was the point of being shy now?

"Lie down on your back."

I did as he said and looked up at him, expecting him to lie on top of me. He didn't. Instead, he scraped his teeth across the inside of my thigh. I spread my legs, opening for him, and I didn't hold back the needy sounds that came with every touch.

"Please, Jett." I sounded as desperate as I felt, and I didn't care.

He smiled at me, a wicked grin, and lowered his head between my legs. His tongue was wet and warm in my folds, and flicked up to my clit. A wave of heat rushed over me.

More. I needed more.

He touched my opening, and added pressure to my clit I didn't know I needed. I squeezed the blanket in my fingers and tilted my head back. Sunlight poured down on me through the tops of the trees, and I tilted my hips into him, restless and close, so close.

He pressed in, and I let go, my tunnel pulsing around him. He sat up and licked his finger. Holy mother of fucking bananas, that was hot.

I sat up, my whole body both charged and satiated at the same time.

He smiled, a dark predatory look in his eyes. "That was only one. You weren't planning on being done now, were you?"

"No." Hell no. I dove at him in an attempt to tackle him to the ground. Yes, he'd made me come, but I wanted his cock.

He didn't fall over, though. He caught me instead. My breasts heaved against his chest, and his cock stood up between us. I reached down and wrapped my fingers around him. A bolt of excitement shot straight to my pussy as I started moving my hand. My body ached to know his.

He held me, and kissed me hard. "Ready for more, are you?"

"Yes."

He flipped me on my back, this time leaning over me, his cock poised at my entrance. He grabbed a condom from his pants and slipped it on. I wrapped my legs up over his hips and pulled his tip inside. He was big, and warm, and smooth. This was where he belonged, this was how we were meant to be.

He reached between us and cupped my breast, flicking the nipple as he gave me what I wanted, pushing inside with one hard stroke. His cock was huge, too big, too hard. He pulled back and gave it to me again, this time there was more, and I stretched for him.

"You okay?" He kissed my cheek, the perfect softness to complement the intensity.

"Yes." My voice was a breathy whisper, the best that I could manage.

He set the pace with a hand on my hip, pulling me to take all of him. And I did. It was the best fucking thing I'd ever experienced, a lifetime leading to this moment, to him, to us. Friction built as he started moving faster, and as amazing as it felt, I didn't want it to be over. Not yet, not ever.

I looked at his strong arms, at his hard chest, to the black ink that decorated his skin. I wanted to learn every line, every picture, every muscle. I took a mental picture, never wanting to forget this moment, the image of him here with me. His eyes were intense, his jaw hard, his hair wild. He was so fucking perfect. How was this man my mate? It didn't matter, because he was. And he wanted me.

His arms and neck tensed. He was watching my face intently. "Come for me, Paige."

And just like that, my body obeyed his words. Pleasure coursed through me, and I cried out. "Bite me, Jett."

His teeth pierced the crook of my neck, a sharp sting that meant so much. I felt the heat of him let go with me, felt his body tense with mine, as one. As my body settled, realization flooded my brain. We were mates. We didn't just both know, but he'd marked me. And I'd asked him to do it. I touched his mark, held it, as if it would disappear if I didn't.

"You okay?" He looked at my hand.

"Yeah, I'm good."

Jett slowly pulled out and rolled onto his side. He slipped the condom off and set it on the corner of the blanket.

I nodded toward the condom. "And now it's a picnic."

He laughed, a light and pleasant sound. Everything had changed, and I could tell he felt it, too.

"Speaking of," Jett sat up and grabbed the basket. "I did pack us some food."

I propped my head in my palm and openly admired the way his shoulders flexed when he moved his arms. The way his abs looked when he was sitting. I was pretty sure I could stare at those all day forever and never get my fill. That wasn't just the abs though, it was all of him. "What do you have?"

He pulled out some french bread and some sliced tomato, pesto, and mozzarella.

"Wow," I nodded and sat up beside him. "Just like everything about you, that is not what I expected."

His eyes danced with amusement. "What exactly did you expect?"

"From Mr. Big and Burly Wolf? Meat."

"You need some meat? I aim to please my mate."

My body flushed at that word coming from his lips. *Mate.* Well, from the word, and from the sight of his still hard cock aimed at me. "I think I've had all the meat I can handle for now."

He laughed. "We'll see how you feel after you've eaten."

"Seriously? You're ready to go again?"

"Always."

"No fucking way."

He tilted his hips, showing me just how big and hard he was. Wow. Yep, maybe he was right. I didn't sense a lie, either.

Best sex of my life—check! Insatiable mate whose libido left me slightly intimidated—check. Couldn't stop smiling —check.

I popped a piece of cheese in my mouth and rose to my feet.

So he liked me naked, enough to promise me forever, but there was still a big first that needed to happen while we had some alone time left.

"Going somewhere?" Jett set down the food, his eyes never leaving me.

"Play with me." I closed my eyes and called to my inner bear. Fur sprouted across my skin and my bones reshaped. The bear was as much a part of me as the curvy girl was, and before the day was over, I wanted him to see me as both. To accept me as both.

Without hesitation, Jett hopped up from the blanket and shifted along side of me. Just like his human form, his wolf was a creature of lithe perfection. His fur was glossy gray, his form larger than the wolves of nature. But me, I was a bear— twice his size.

The bear wasn't the most feminine of animals, but it was who I was. I was big, I was strong, and maybe a little bit awkward, too. That had more to do with me than my bear, though. Every other bear shifter I'd met had seemed well suited to the form.

Jett circled around me, and I wished I could read his thoughts. When he reached my front once again, he flicked his tail across my nose and bounded into the stream. I ran after him, splashing into the icy water. It sprayed up onto my legs, soaking my fur. The mud beneath my paws was soft and pleasant.

I swiped a leg, spraying water all over Jett. He shook his fur, splashing me right back.

This was better than anything I'd ever imagined. Too good to be true. And if it was just a dream, I never wanted to wake up.

CHAPTER SIXTEEN

JETT

I hadn't stopped thinking about my picnic with Paige since I'd dropped her off. Not during the night, and not this morning. I couldn't get the image of her naked form out of my head. Hell, I didn't want to. There was a primal need ruling my brain, one that had only grown stronger since I'd tasted her once. I wanted to be inside of her again and again, to feel her body pressed to mine and never let go.

Paige bent down to refill her paint roller with another layer of yellow, offering me the perfect view of her round ass. Her jean shorts lifted, revealing the curve at the top of her thighs. I wanted to grab hold of her hips and sink my cock into her, just like that, right here in my old bedroom. But now wasn't the time. And this room was about to belong to my daughter.

Evelyn shook my arm. I looked down.

"Like this?" She turned the screwdriver awkwardly in her hands.

"Almost." I adjusted her grip and put my hand over hers

and twisted the screw, tightening the two boards together. "This way."

We were getting our home ready, as a family. That was nice, too, and what I needed to focus on. Because *I had a family.*

"Can I do this one?" Evelyn picked up the last screw.

"Yeah, go ahead."

She went down to the other end of the bed frame, and this time, started screwing it in the right way.

"How's it going, Evie?" Paige stretched up on her toes and rolled a fresh coat of paint down the wall.

"Good." Her voice strained as she put her full weight into twisting the handle. She flopped down on the floor. "I think I did it."

"Let's check that out and see." I bent down beside her. "Screwdriver, please."

She set it in my palm, and I tested the joint. It was loose, but at least she hadn't stripped the screw.

"So, Dad, how'd I do?"

"You did great." I patted her shoulder.

She beamed, a wide grin, and I noticed a gap where a tooth was missing. A pang of regret hit me. We could have shared these kinds of moments all along. She'd been mine since the day she was born, but I'd missed out on so many firsts—her first steps, her first words, her first lost tooth, and countless other milestones I didn't know about because I wasn't there. Did she believe in the Tooth Fairy? Santa? All the stories of magic that people usually told their children? We hadn't celebrated those types of things growing up, but suddenly I wanted to. I wanted to see Evelyn experience the wonder that I hadn't.

I looked at Paige, who was still busy painting. Did she know the answers to my questions? Did she have pictures from the milestones I'd missed? The birthday parties I'd never been to? The games I'd never seen my daughter play? My heart ached with a strange sense of loss, for all the time I hadn't known my daughter.

"You used to live with your grandma, right?" I asked Evelyn.

Paige looked over.

"Yep," Evelyn said. "But it's more fun here."

"I'm glad." I tapped her knee. "Are there still things in your old room that you'd like to have here when it's ready?"

"You mean I get to bring my favorite stuffed animals with me?" Evelyn's eyes went wide with surprise.

I looked to Paige.

Paige said, "I bet we could arrange a time do a pick-up with Aunt Sylvia—"

"Yes!" Evelyn through her fists up in victory.

"After the kitchen and the bathroom are done." Paige arched her brow and gave Evelyn a pointed look.

Evelyn's shoulders dropped. "How long is *that* going to take?

Both of them turned to me. Oh, my turn to answer.

"A couple of weeks."

"That's forever." Evelyn collapsed back down onto the carpet. "What if it's time to go back to school before it's done? Am I going back to the same school?"

Her wide eyes assessed first Paige, then me.

"When school starts up, you'll go to Ashwood Elementary," I said.

It was another change, one that might be harder to take than some of the others.

Even though I expected tears, when her eyes glassed over, it still felt like shit. Moving was one of the most stressful events in a person's life, and she was only a child. A child who had been moving around a lot lately. I searched for the right words to make her feel better, but knowing what to say had never been my strong suit. When shit hit the fan, and Hawke was taking it badly, I'd punch him in the arm and tell him not to be a pussy. I was pretty sure that wasn't going to work here, so I was lost.

"You'll make new friends." Paige set the roller down and sat down beside Evelyn. "And it's going to be great, because here you'll have a place to bring them back to hang out."

"In the tree house?"

"If it's safe," Paige nodded.

"And in my new room?"

"I don't see why not."

Evelyn gave Paige a quick hug. "Do you think I could bring Lacey over? As soon as it's ready?" She gasped. "Do you think she'll go to my school?

Lacey was Shaundra's daughter. I was really glad the girls were getting along so well.

"She will." I nodded.

Evelyn squealed. "I hope we're in the same class."

"Even if you're not, I'm sure you'll see her on the playground and at the cafeteria," Paige offered.

Evelyn nodded her head and narrowed her eyes. "Yeah, that would be good, too. But it's better if we're in the same class."

"Of course." Paige smiled.

I still needed to figure out what I had to do to get Evelyn enrolled. And into what grade.

The burner phone I was using until mine was recovered buzzed in my pocket. I reached down and checked the screen. Hawke.

H: *We need to talk. In person.*

SHIT. There was still time to figure out school later, after the conflict with Greenville was settled. There'd be time for all of this. I didn't want to go back and deal with whatever the newest problem was, but it was my duty.

As much as I hated to end my time with Paige and Evelyn, I couldn't ignore Hawke.

J: Back soon.

I SLIPPED my phone back in my pocket. "Okay, ladies, it's time to wrap up and call it a day."

"What?" Evelyn wrinkled her nose and shook her head. "It's not even lunchtime yet. How are we supposed to get everything ready if we aren't here?"

"The house'll be ready soon, I promise." I rose to my feet.

Paige was staring, unmoving, her eyes questioning.

"Can we come back tomorrow?" Evelyn asked. "First thing as soon as I wake up? I can wake up real early, before the sun. I don't even have to sleep!"

"You should sleep," I said. "You need rest to grow big and strong."

"Oh, I'm already strong."

"I know," I said. "You did great work today. You couldn't have done those screws if you weren't strong."

"How about after dinner we come back? It's close to morning. And if I don't sleep, it's the same."

"Time to pack up, Evie." Paige's voice was kind but firm. She cleaned up the painting supplies without even looking at me.

I wanted to grab her, pull her against my chest, and tell her everything was fine. She and Evelyn were what mattered most in the world to me. I just had to check in on something. But I couldn't promise everything was fine until I'd met with Hawke. And I wouldn't lie to her.

Paige walked by me with the roller tray, giving a wide berth. She was pissed and I couldn't blame her. She was staying in Ashwood for me, at my assurance that everything would be fine. And what if I couldn't promise her that?

The three of us rode back to the bed and breakfast in relative silence. Silence save for Evelyn humming and making neighing sounds in the back seat as she made Mr. Stabbyface bounce around with her unicorn.

Paige's shoulders were tense, and her jaw was tight. I needed to say something to make this right. She parked along the curb, turned off the car, and we all climbed out. Evie skipped her way up the stairs and opened the door before looking back for Paige.

"You go ahead in," Paige said. "I'll be there in a minute."

"Okay. Bye, Dad." Evelyn waved.

"See ya, squirt."

The door clicked shut and Paige let out a sigh before puffing her chest up and meeting me at the front of the car. I could see that spark in her fierce walnut eyes that meant she was about to tell me what a piece of shit I was being. It was a look I knew well, one many women had given me before. But Paige wasn't just any woman. She was my mate, so it meant more.

I pulled her in, and her breath caught as I parted her lips with mine.

She tasted sweet and salty. She tasted like she was mine. She opened for me, and she arched her back, melding her body against me. I wanted to take her there on the hood of her car, leave my mark on her all over again, relive the connection we'd shared the day before.

She broke our kiss and looked up at me. "Jett, you really—"

"I love you, Paige. You and Evelyn are what matters most to me."

She frowned, but said nothing, and instead looked down.

"Hey." I tilted her chin up with a gentle touch of my finger.

She met my gaze, and her eyes glossed over. "It's trouble with that other pack again, isn't it?"

"I don't know yet."

"I need this to be over, so we can start our life together."

"That's what I want, too."

"Good," she said, and pulled away. "Remember that when you get there. Think of us when you decide what you do next."

The door opened just before she reached it, and Evelyn was standing there with a smug grin. "You *kissed* my dad, Aunt Paige. You *love* him."

Paige's face turned red and a hint of a smile played on her lips. "Come on, munchkin, let's go upstairs."

With that, the door shut, and I was alone. I drove back to the clubhouse on my bike, Paige's words echoing through my head. Of course I would think of them. I never stopped thinking about them. Paige and Evelyn were my heart.

I parked and went in through the back. Shaundra looked up at me from her place behind the bar, and lifted a brow. She pulled the earbud out of one of her ears. "He's waiting for you in the boardroom. And he's pissed."

"Thanks for the warning." I headed down the hall to the business side of the building.

I could hear Brick's muffled voice through the closed door. "Want me to hunt his ass down and drag him here?"

I grabbed the handle and stepped inside. "If you're talking about me, no need."

The air was thick and cold, tension running high. Brick was in his chair, feet up on the table, and Hawke was pacing. He froze and met my gaze. "About fucking time."

I crossed the room and took my usual seat across from Brick. "I came as quickly as I could."

"You picked a hell of a time to get distracted." Hawke took his seat at the head of the table.

"We needed you. Or at least this guy thought we did." Brick nodded toward Hawke. "Me, I told him I could handle this on my own."

Hawke's attention remained on me. I could see the wheels turning in his head, and that set me more on edge than Brick's sinister grin.

Since it seemed no one was going to tell me what the hell was going on, I asked. "Why am I here?"

Brick slid a phone across the table. The screen was cracked. "Is that mine?"

Brick nodded. "Found it. And my keys."

"Good." I nodded and grabbed my broken phone from the table. The screen would need to be fixed at the very least. Could be the thing was completely busted. But that wasn't what was important. What the hell had happened when they found the guy whose trunk this was in?

"We need you to ID the driver," Hawke said.

"Do you have pictures?" I asked.

"Better." Brick's face split from ear to ear. "I have him downstairs."

Fuck. This was bad. Worse than I'd thought.

"Fine," I said. "Show me."

I followed Brick, with Hawke a few steps behind me.

The scent of blood hit me before we reached the basement. Blood and piss.

Greenville wouldn't stand for us taking their man, as much as I knew Hawke wouldn't stand for what was done to me. Not to mention the crimes committed against the roving chapter.

In the center of the room was a man chained to one of the support beams. By scent, I knew he was a wolf shifter. His body sagged against the floor, but his heart still beat.

I circled around, keeping my distance from him, until I got a look at his face. It was swollen and bruised, but I still recognized him.

"This is the man who was driving the car," Brick said. "He won't tell me his name...yet. But we're just getting started." He took a step forward, and Hawke grabbed his wrist.

"Tell me, Jett. Is this the man from the Briggs building?"

"No." I knew without question he wasn't. This guy had dirty-blond hair, not black. And he was smaller than smashed-face Tiny, too. This was his accomplice.

"That's bullshit." Brick's voice boomed, and the chained man curled his body at the sound. "Your scent is all over his fucking shoes."

"He wasn't the one who drugged me," I said. I didn't take this admission lightly. I didn't want any more bloodshed. But I wouldn't lie to Hawke. "He was there when I woke up. He helped."

Brick laughed. "I fucking knew it."

This is what the Butchers used to be. It wasn't who we were supposed to be anymore. As much as I hated this man for what he did to me, he was just a soldier following orders. He didn't make the call.

"Don't kill him." I clasped Brick's shoulder.

"Seriously?" He raised a brow. "I wouldn't. After what he did, you should have the honor."

I looked to Hawke. He seemed lost in thought, staring at the man on the floor. I didn't want this. I didn't want any of this. I wanted a peaceful life in the cabin with my family. I wanted to do the right thing, and I knew deep down, Hawke did, too.

"There's still a way to walk away from this," I said.

"Great," Hawke said. "I'm open to ideas."

I couldn't peel my eyes off of the broken man on the floor. I'd already tried to talk to Briggs. We'd need to think of something else, but what?

"Let me think on it," I said. "And Brick, leave him be."

He looked to Hawke, and Hawke nodded. Brick stomped up the stairs, grumbling under his breath.

Hawke clasped my shoulder. "Think fast, brother."

CHAPTER SEVENTEEN

PAIGE

I t started as an article about pants. While I still maintained that soft spot in my heart for being comfortable, that was not the story I wanted to tell. The story that spoke to me was the not so graceful tale of falling in love. A story about a girl from the city who found everything she was looking for, and more, in someone she'd expected to hate. But even though I'd found my mate, and I was sure he was the one for me, this didn't feel like the happily ever after I'd dreamed about. Reality was filled with bumps in the road.

I stared at my screen, trying not to listen to Evie reading her library book to her stuffed animals.

Love is attraction and acceptance. It's splashing in the stream, and it's the best sex of your life. It's knowing that forever is within your grasp, and knowing you've found the person you want to share that forever with.

It's a cabin in the woods, with a dark past and a fresh coat of paint. But what about when the darkness seeps through, when your view of the future is clouded and murky? When it's so dark that you don't know whether you're swimming or drowning?

YEAH, no. I was running out of time to get this thing done, and if I couldn't, I guessed it was going to be an article about pants after all. That wasn't the worst thing that could happen, but what did that mean about me? If I couldn't tell a story about a happily ever after, did I really get to have one? Maybe reality didn't just mean bumps in the road, but that there was no ending where everything was peachy sunshine and rainbows. Maybe it was just life, and life was about making decisions. Sometimes ones that worked out, and sometimes not.

I noticed it was quiet. A little too quiet. I looked over to Evie, who was staring at me from her seat on the floor.

"Are you going to marry my dad?"

"Uh..." I hadn't really thought about it, but given Marla was human, Evie probably didn't know anything about shifters. It seemed like a parent discussion, like the birds and the bees.

I guessed as acting female caretaker, that meant it was my job. What the hell was I supposed to say?

"I have a secret," I said. It was something, I guessed.

"I like secrets. Can I guess? You *already did* marry my dad!"

"Good guess," I said. "But no."

She pushed out her pouty lip.

"I have a secret that is about me. And it's also about your dad. And you, too."

"Okay." She ran over to the bed and jumped up beside me.

I closed my laptop and considered what to say next. "You

know in your story where the girl turns into a unicorn, with magic?"

"Yeah, of course."

"It's kind of like that."

"No way. You're not a unicorn." She sounded uncertain.

"Not a unicorn."

"Are you trying to trick me?"

"I swear I'm not." I offered her my pinky, and we shook on it. "Have you ever heard of shifters?"

Evie shrugged. "Are they *like* unicorns?"

"A little." I put my arm around her shoulder. "Shifters are people, but they have a secret."

"Like you have a secret."

"Exactly. It's something we can't talk about with anyone who doesn't share that same secret."

"Okay…"

I seemed to be losing her a little. This was harder than I'd thought it would be. "I'm not going to marry your dad, because that's not our way."

"But I saw you kiss."

"Yeah," I said. "But, shifters don't get married. Generally. They find a mate, and they spend their lives together, but they don't do the whole wedding thing."

"I don't understand."

"Hmmm…I don't turn into a unicorn. I turn into a bear."

"No way. That's just pretend."

"It's real. And your dad, he turns into a wolf."

"What?" She gave me a look that said she thought I was full of shit.

"And one day you'll be able to turn into a wolf, too."

"I don't think so."

"It's true. But it's also a secret. So you can't tell anyone about it who isn't a shifter. It's rule number one."

"What are the other rules?"

Maybe I should have thought that out. I shrugged. "I don't know. But that's a big one."

"So I can't talk to Lacey?"

"Actually, you can. Because she's a shifter, too. It's like a secret club we're all in together."

"That doesn't sound bad."

"It's not bad at all." I smiled down at her. Maybe this wasn't going as terrible as I'd thought.

"Can I see?"

"See what?"

"See you become a bear? How am I supposed to believe you if I don't see?"

Fair question. "Next time we go out in the woods, I'll show you."

"If it's not a trick, why won't you show me now?"

"The rest of the people in town, they aren't all shifters. Especially the ones staying in this building. We don't want to scare them, right?"

"I guess not."

"Do you think a big bear would scare them?"

"Yeah."

"Well, okay then. We'll wait for the woods." Yes, parenting win. I gave myself a mental high five.

"Paige?" she said.

"Yes, Evie?"

"If you and my dad are mates, does that make you my new mom?"

My chest swelled and tears filled my eyes. "I'd like that very much."

"I think I would, too."

She threw her arms around my neck, and I squeezed her back. It felt good to hug her, to hug my friend's daughter, who was becoming my daughter. I loved Evie. That was easy. Part of me wondered what Marla would think of all of this if she could see us. Would she be happy for me and for Evie? I hoped so.

"I have an idea," I said as she let go.

"What is it?"

"Let's see if we can make an appointment to check out your new school, and maybe even see Lacey. I bet she can tell you all kinds of things about the teachers and the other kids."

"And about shifters."

"That, too." I nodded.

"Yay! Can we eat first? I'm hungry."

"Yep, we can definitely do that."

We grabbed some food downstairs, perfect timing, and I called Shaundra. She offered to meet us at the school, and even called to get us all a walkthrough appointment. Evie didn't stop bouncing from the time we finished eating to when we arrived at the school.

The tour was nice, and Evie had a great time with Lacey showing her everything. The woman from the front office gave me a bunch of forms, and we went out to the playground when it was over. I found myself too distracted to take much of any of it in, and I had nothing to compare the experience to except for school when I was a kid. This place had the same smell. Maybe all elementary schools did. I didn't even know I remembered what my old school smelled like until I'd walked the halls here, but it was true.

Shaundra and I sat together on a bench while Lacey and Evie ran around the playground.

"What did you think?" Shaundra asked.

"It seems nice."

"First time with this kind of thing?"

"Is it that obvious?"

She smiled. "It can be overwhelming. I remember that with my oldest. All the forms, and the questions about what they know and what they don't know. But in the end, it'll be fine."

"Yeah, I guess it will."

Her eyes flicked to the mark on my neck, then back to my face. "Are you worried about Jett? You two are mated now, right?"

"Yeah," I said, kind of answering both questions with just the one word.

"He'll keep Hawke straight. And everything'll be fine."

"What do you mean?"

She searched my face and then cringed. "Maybe I shouldn't have said that. I just assumed...I'm sure everything will be fine."

"What do I need to know?" I asked. "I'm his mate, Shaundra."

I was going for strong, but my voice sounded strained, desperate.

She gave me a small smile and tapped my hand. "Hawke's a good guy. He relies on Jett, and always has, to be his moral compass."

"Shouldn't he have one of those of his own?"

She laughed. "He does, I'm sure. But when there's trouble, Brick wants to act. Jett's that balancing force for Hawke, the one who tells him to think first."

I sighed. I guessed it was good that my man was the one with sense, but I was so tired of this rollercoaster of emotions already. And still, I had no idea what was going on. So I pressed Shaundra. "What kind of trouble?"

"I, uh...you should ask Jett about that."

I folded my hands in my lap and stared down at me feet. "We hardly know each other," I said. "You've known him longer. What kind of man is he?"

"A good one. He used to be a prick, like the rest of them,

but never as much as the rest of them. No matter what happens, I'm sure he'll be there for you and Evelyn."

I hoped she was right. Part of me was entirely certain that at his core, Jett was the man that he showed us when we were working as a family on the cabin, and somehow also the playful commander who'd rocked my world in the woods. But what scared me was the part he didn't share. What was he doing now? What kind of man was he when he wasn't with us? I hated that he was trying to deal with whatever the hell kind of trouble Shaundra was talking about without sharing it with me. I hated that I didn't know what he was trying to shield me from. Was I ever going to get all of him? Or just the pieces he wanted to share?

"Look at me, Paige!" Evie waved from the top of the slide before riding down.

"Wow," I said. "That's a fast slide."

"Let's go again." Lacey grabbed her hand and the two girls giggled.

Shaundra gave me a sad smile and checked her phone. I didn't need to check mine. I knew Jett wasn't going to reach out, not while he was busy with his pack, with the part of his life that he kept hidden.

CHAPTER EIGHTEEN

JETT

Fuck the Greenville Pack. Fuck Brick. Fuck this damned war.

The plastic bag stretched and puckered as I dumped the contents of my drawers inside. One more bag for bedding, and the room was bare. Hell of a life, summed up in two trash bags. The thought left a bitter taste on my tongue.

The Silent Butchers were my past. Paige and Evelyn were my future.

The house wasn't ready, but we'd make do. It was safest if we were together. It was the only way I could protect them. No question, Greenville was coming. It was only a matter of when.

Before Brick had taken one of theirs, I'd thought the bed and breakfast was far enough from the clubhouse that this shit wouldn't reach them. But now, I'd be surprised if Briggs didn't scour the whole fucking town.

I took my bags out and strapped them to my bike. The plastic bulged unevenly off the back of the seat. It would hold long enough to make it to the cabin, which was all that mattered.

I heard the door to the clubhouse open behind me. My shoulders tensed as I finished tightening the straps. It had to be Brick, coming out to give me shit about leaving.

"Jett."

My shoulders dropped. It wasn't Brick. It was Hawke. I turned to face my best friend, my alpha, my brother.

"You're leaving?" His face was hard, and his voice was quiet.

I felt like an ass for hurting him. I wanted to help, but I couldn't risk being away from my family when the Greenville City Pack attacked.

"I have to be with my daughter and my mate."

Recognition flashed in his eyes. "You found your mate?"

"Yeah, Paige. She's a bear shifter." I couldn't believe I hadn't told him. We weren't exactly chatty, but life-changing shit—I should have told him. I guessed we hadn't really spent any time together since it happened.

"Cheers."

"Thanks, brother." Paige and Evelyn changed everything for me. But they changed nothing about the situation here for the MC.

He nodded. "You're afraid."

"Hell, yeah, I'm afraid. For the first time in my life I have something to lose, and I'm fucking terrified."

Hawke clenched his hands into fists. "I need a plan, and I need you here."

"I wish I could be." And I did. I hated to leave him to deal with this shit, but my family had to come first.

"You want out of the pack?" Hawke's eyes were hard. I'd hurt him, and he was pissed enough to throw a punch. If he did, I'd understand.

"No."

"I never should have sent you to The Meat Locker to speak to Draper." His shoulders sank and he looked out at the setting sun in the distance, over the mountains and trees. "I shouldn't have let you go to Greenville to talk to Briggs."

I laid a hand on Hawke's shoulder. "This shit started with the roving chapter. It wasn't your doing. Even if I'd never talked to Draper, Briggs still could have been coming after us. There's no way to know."

"What the hell am I supposed to do?"

He didn't want a war. He didn't want to fight. Hawke had worked damned hard at steering the Ashwood Chapter of the Silent Butchers to the right side of the law. We both had. And everything was about to go to shit, over something someone else did.

"You don't have to fight," I said. "Call the other chapters, tell them about Greenville. Let someone deal with them that still wants the life."

Hawke's mouth flattened into a line, and he furrowed his brow. It wasn't the first time I'd thought about suggesting that the pack drop the MC label since we'd gone straight, but I hadn't said anything.

"Maybe it's time to let the club go," I continued. "I know I'm ready. We're already a pack. We don't have to be Butchers, too."

The words burned in my throat even as I said them, aching in my chest like the death of a loved one. That didn't make it any less true. Pain was inevitable. Happiness required work.

"You might be ready," he said, "but I don't know that I am."

"That's okay, too." I offered my hand for a shake before leaving. Hawke took it and pulled me in. He tapped my back before stepping away. We were still family, and he wasn't pissed. I couldn't believe he wasn't pissed.

"Where will you go?" he asked.

"The cabin."

The look he gave me said I hadn't mentioned that either. "Your parents' place."

"I'm fixing it up."

He slapped my shoulder. "Never thought you'd set foot in that house voluntarily again."

I nodded. "Things change."

He took a step back. "So it seems."

I climbed on my bike, sure this was the right thing to do, the only thing I could do. And it hurt like hell. Feeling the weight of his gaze on me, part of me wanted to go back inside. But I couldn't. It was time to move on.

I drove away feeling like a fucking prick. There was more I should have said. I should have promised I'd still be there for my job, to deal with all the legal work with the security business. I should have told him that we were still brothers, no matter what.

No, he had enough to deal with right now. We could talk later. He had my number, and he knew where to find me. After shit settled, I'd reach out if I hadn't heard from him.

Right now, I needed to claim my future and retrieve my family.

I pulled up to the curb by the bed and breakfast, but Paige's silver sedan wasn't there. Better to wait than drive around hunting for her, so I parked my bike and took a seat on the porch step.

There was movement in the window above me. A woman peered out before closing the curtain. I recognized her from before as the woman who owned the place.

Streetlamps flicked on one at a time, like keys pressed on a piano. The evening glow would soon pass, the quiet street falling into darkness. Where was Paige?

A rogue thought crossed my mind—what if I was too late? I knew it was stupid. If Greenville was already here, they'd be headed to the clubhouse, not to a bed and breakfast a few blocks away.

But that didn't make me feel any better.

The door behind me opened. "You coming in?"

"I'm just waiting for someone," I said, without turning around.

"In the dark? Your girlfriend will find you inside just as well as she would out here. I've even got a chair by the window for you to do your brooding in."

Ha. I liked this woman already.

"I'm good, thanks."

"Fine, but don't cry at me when someone coming in or out falls on top of you."

No one else was around. My guess was Paige was the only one staying here, anyway. Still, if the woman wanted to pretend, there was no harm done.

"I won't," I said.

She went back in, and before long, a set of headlights approached. They were here.

I rose to my feet and headed over to the curb as Paige parked.

She threw open her door and climbed out. "What's wrong?"

"Nothing."

I regretted the lie as soon as it left my lips. I didn't want to worry her, or Evelyn.

"Bullshit." Paige looked to my bike, at the bags attached, then back at me. "Truth. Now."

Better to tell her than to fight. "I want you and Evelyn to come with me to the cabin."

"What, right now? What happened to finishing the kitchen and bathroom first?"

I heard Evelyn's soft voice from inside the car. It was laced with concern. "Is everything okay?"

KEIRA BLACKWOOD

"Everything's fine, Evie," Paige replied. She reached into the car and shut off the engine. Then she shut the door and put her hands on her hips.

I opened the back and Evelyn jumped out at me, wrapping her arms around my waist. "Dad! I'm so glad you're here."

"I'm glad to be here," I said. "Want to try out your new bedroom tonight?"

"Yes!" She jumped up and down. "I just need to get Mr. Stabbyface and Pokey first."

"Pokey?"

"My unicorn!"

I could feel Paige glaring at me, her eyes two flaming balls of fury.

"Go ahead in. We need to get packed," I said to Evelyn. Her blond hair bounced and she skipped to the door.

Paige stepped in front of me and poked my chest.

"This is not okay. You don't get to show up and make demands without talking to me."

"I thought you liked when I commanded you."

I'd expected a laugh or a smile. My words seemed to have the opposite effect.

"Seriously? No. Tell me the fucking truth right now or Evie and I are staying put. You can go. We won't. No lies, Jett."

She was so upset, and that was the opposite of my intention. I wanted her not to worry.

I reached out and touched her shoulders, easing the tension. I ran my palms down her arms, pulling her hands from her hips. "Right now, everything *is* okay. I just want to be cautious. I would feel better if I knew you two were safely with me, outside of town."

Her brown eyes softened, anger fading to concern. "Okay."

"Okay?" After her initial reaction, I didn't expect it to be so easy.

"I trust you. We'll come with you to the cabin."

"Great. I thought I might have to tie you up and carry you."

She raised a brow and there was a hint of amusement playing in her eyes. "Is that what you thought?"

"I hadn't thought much about it, really. But I am now. I think you might just like that."

Paige's gaze flicked over to the window, where Evelyn was watching us.

"I still want the whole story. But for now, let's go inside and you can help us pack."

Everything was going to be okay. We'd be together in the cabin, and I'd keep my family safe.

CHAPTER NINETEEN

PAIGE

*L*eaning on the frame, I watched over Evie from her bedroom doorway. The paint had only just dried, the bed was just built, and here we were moving into the cabin. It felt like a new house, even without everything complete like Jett had wanted. But that wasn't what bothered me. It was the rushing to get us here that left me uneasy.

By the way Evie was sleeping, she didn't seem to share my concern. Her chest rose and fell softly, her expression relaxed. In her arms were the unicorn I'd given her and the rhino that had belonged to Jett. I hadn't seen her rest so peacefully since...well, ever.

A warm sensation washed over me as the scent of spiced cider enveloped me. I couldn't hear Jett's approach, but I could feel it. A moment later, he leaned over my shoulder, the rough hair of his beard scratching my ear and sending a shiver down my spine.

"Come to bed." He wrapped his hand around my hip, and warmth coiled out from his touch.

My first thought was to nod emphatically, follow him to the bed, and strip naked. My second thought was to protest.

We still needed to talk about what was going on, and I couldn't afford to get distracted by his big hands or his cool breath on my neck. I crossed my arms, making a stand, even if it was only half-hearted.

I turned to him, and found his face hidden in shadow. Even though the hall was dark, I could still make out his features, but I couldn't read his expression.

"I don't want to wake her." His voice was a whisper, but somehow still deep and rough. This man could tenderize meat with that voice...tenderize me.

"We need to talk," I whispered back, maintaining my resolve.

He nodded and gestured for me to lead the way. Had I read him wrong? It seemed like he wanted to talk too.

I stepped into the master bedroom, *our bedroom,* and took a seat on the edge of the bed, *our bed.* I'd never lived with a guy before. This was uncharted territory. It left me hopeful and uneasy at the same time. I wanted to enjoy all of our firsts, to appreciate the little moments that were the start of our life together, but there was a dark cloud hanging over us, tainting everything. Even if there wasn't, this didn't *feel* like home. It didn't smell like home, either. Not yet, at least. It would take actually having my own belongings here, and Evie's. And it would take time.

Jett shut the door and turned to me. I watched as he toed off his shoes and unfastened his pants. Part of me wanted to tell him to stop, that being pantsless was dangerous business. But we could talk in bed without pants. It didn't have to mean we weren't going to talk.

He emptied his pockets onto the dresser and dropped his jeans in the hamper. I may have been staring at the way his ass looked in those boxers. And maybe I wasn't. But I definitely noticed his package when he sat down beside me. I couldn't even try to deny that.

Jett laced his fingers in mine on the comforter. My breath caught in my chest. Would he always have this effect on me?

"How are you holding up?" His deep blue eyes sucked me in, and I couldn't look away.

"Okay," I said. I blinked hard, trying to break the spell. "No, not okay. I need to know what's going on."

"One of the guys fucked up." He looked away. "With the Butchers engaging...I don't know if it can end peacefully."

Leave, I thought. *Leave the Silent Butchers.* But I couldn't say the words. It wasn't fair. This was his family we were talking about.

"I told Hawke to let the MC go."

"What?"

"Being a part of the Ashwood Pack should be enough. I don't want the shit that other chapters do to fall down on...my family." He looked at me and a flutter of hope filled my chest.

"What did Hawke say?" It seemed like too much to expect, too easy a way out. I always thought motorcycle clubs had a til-death-do-you-serve policy, like a really fucked-up marriage.

"Nothing."

"That sucks." He must have had no idea what his friend was thinking. Harder than getting out, was probably convincing a bunch of die-hard bikers to just let it all go.

"Yeah."

"But you're still part of the pack, right?" Stepping away shouldn't change that. Well, for Jett's sake, I hoped it didn't.

"*We* are."

"Me?" I already had familial bonds to another group of shifters, back in Frozen Peaks. But it wasn't like I actually wanted to belong there. I'd given up that dream before I'd finished grade school.

"You're my mate. You and Evelyn are part of the pack

now." A sad smile crossed his face. "So long as you want to be."

Why wouldn't I want to be? I wanted everything with Jett. I wanted to know the people he cared about, to be a part of his life. At least, part of a *safe* life. "Of course I do. If the rest of them are anything like Shaundra, I'll be lucky to know them, and even luckier to call them family."

"It's settled then. Welcome to the Ashwood Pack, *Paige Greyson.*"

We hadn't talked about changing my last name, but it had a finality to it, one that made me giddy. "Thank you, *Jett Greyson.*"

His thumb flicked over my palm, and his eyes darkened, revealing the predator within. My breathing quickened in response.

In one quick movement, he pulled me onto his lap, capturing me in his embrace. His hard cock pressed up between us, barely covered by the thin cotton of his boxers. It seemed this time I had him at a disadvantage, me completely clothed, him partially unwrapped for me.

"I want to make you come in every room, so all I can think about when I'm in this place is the little whimpers that you make, the image of your bare skin. So all I can remember is the taste of you on my tongue." His lips captured mine as he held me flush against his chest.

As hot as it was, my heart broke for him that he needed new memories to overwrite the bad, that home had never been a warm fuzzy feeling for him. But my childhood wasn't something I looked back on in a positive light, either.

As his tongue caressed mine, as I ran my hands over his massive arms, I realized—these were the memories I wanted, too. Home could be the place we fucked, the place we made love, the memory of his commands and his sweetness. It wasn't a place at all. Home was Jett.

I rose to my feet and tore off my shorts. I wanted those memories to start here, in our new bed. And I wanted them to start now.

Jett stood with me and lifted the hem of my shirt. His fingers brushed over my stomach, a touch of contact that left me wanting more. Heat pooled in my core. We needed this. I needed him.

His lips were soft, his hands gentle. Last time, I'd wanted rough and fast. I'd been desperate to seal our connection, but this time there wasn't the same urgency. This time, I knew he was mine.

The patterns of ink on his chest were swirled and wild, like the flow of the wind. I followed them with my fingers.

Jett flattened my hand softly over his heart. "I love you, Paige."

"I love you, too."

His lips were soft, his touch gentle as he laid me down on the bed and showed me. He kissed me, he filled me, and together we were one. Soft and slow, deep yet gentle, I didn't want to blink and miss a second of staring into his deep blue eyes. I was lost in him, one with him, forever in love with this man.

The build-up was sweet, and the orgasm was all the better for it. Our fingers laced, our bodies in sync, we found release together. And soon after, contentment and rest.

* * *

"PAIGE." Jett gently shook my shoulder, but it was his tone that startled my eyes open. It was still dark, and it felt like the middle of the night.

"Wha...what is it?"

"Do you smell that?" Jett jumped out of bed and threw on his boxers.

I blinked hard and sat up. "What's going on?"

"Wolves...Protect Evelyn."

"Yeah, of course." My voice sounded totally calm, a robot on auto-response. By the time I climbed out of bed, Jett had already left the room. I threw on underwear and a t-shirt and raced toward Evie. Jett was in the living room, peering through the curtains. I wanted to go to him, to look outside and see what was going on. But I needed to guard Evie.

I found her sleeping peacefully in her bed, totally unaware that something was wrong.

What the fuck was happening? I sat on the edge of her bed, and only then did I realize my hands were trembling.

The air was cool and tinted with the wild scent of shifter. *Wolves.* Jett had said it was wolves, and now that I was awake enough to process, I knew without question he was right.

I tried to tell myself that everything was fine. Jett knew lots of wolves. But if this was a friend, they wouldn't be arriving without notice in the middle of the night. No, this was the trouble Jett had run away from. It had followed us here...right to our doorstep.

There were sounds outside, engines, voices.

"Call Shaundra and don't open the door for anyone," Jett said from the other room. A slam and click told me he was gone.

Let him be okay.

I glanced at Evie, then headed back to the master bedroom. I needed my phone. I grabbed it from the night-stand, then returned to the hall, outside Evie's door, and made the call.

It rang twice before a groggy voice answered. "Hello?"

"Hey, It's Paige. I'm sorry to call so late." What time was it anyway? I pulled the phone from my ear just enough to check. *2:48.* Very late.

"It's okay. What's wrong?" There was a sharpness to her

voice that suggested Shaundra was able to wake up a lot more quickly than I was.

"We're at Jett's cabin. Something's wrong. There are wolves here, and he told me to call you." My voice was shaking. My whole body was shaking.

"Everything's going to be okay. Backup's on the way." With that, she hung up.

I turned around and found Evie in the doorway. I must have been too loud on the phone. Her eyes were hooded, still half-asleep, and her hair was a tangled mess. Her little body swayed, like she might just collapse where she stood.

"Hey, sweetie." I knelt down and steadied her shoulders. "Let's get you back to bed."

"What's happening?"

"Everything's okay." I hoped she couldn't hear the lie in my words. To me, it stood out, though I kept my voice soft and even.

"Where's Dad?"

"Come on." I turned her around, led her back to the bed, and tucked her into the covers.

"Aunt Paige, what's wrong?" The glossiness faded from her eyes as she looked at me.

I forced myself to smile.

"Everything's going to be okay." I sounded like a broken record, a jacked-up sound bite stuck on repeat. I didn't know what else to say.

Deep howls carried through the air, one after another, in every direction.

If anyone tried to get in, I'd shift. I had to protect Evie no matter what.

"Remember how we talked about shifters?" I asked.

She nodded.

"Well, I'm going to show you exactly how it works."

"Like a game?"

"Exactly. It'll be fun. And if anything else happens, you climb under your bed, okay? Don't come out for any reason. Can you do that for me?"

She nodded and pulled the blanket up over half her face. "Aunt Paige?"

"Yeah?"

"I'm scared."

"I know." Could I tell her I was, too? Did I lie and tell her again that everything was okay? I didn't know how I was supposed to handle this. What happened if someone broke the door down? What was I supposed to do if they came in here? I could take one wolf, for sure. Maybe two. But from the howls, it sounded like an entire pack.

The mama bear inside of me was ready for the fight, huffing and teeming at the surface. I wasn't sure that it was the best move. What if Evie was scared by my shift? What if she ran?

I focused, keeping control, and started the shift, just enough for fur to ripple across my skin. Evie squealed and covered her entire head. I shoved the bear back, maintaining human form.

"It's okay," I said. "It's just me, see?"

I tried to peel the blanket down, but Evie held tight. This wasn't working. I didn't want to scare her.

Crash. The window shattered, and I jumped. Evie started crying as the vicious sounds of fighting wolves poured in. I scooped her up in my arms, and she held tight to my neck.

I couldn't stop to think. I couldn't focus on the fact that out there, one of those wolves was my mate.

I ran to the bedroom, slipped on my shoes, grabbed my keys, and ran for the door.

Blood rushed to my head, my heart thundering in my chest. I ran for the car.

"Don't look." My words were as much for me as they were for Evie.

Jett. I climbed through the driver's side, and told Evie to climb into the back. As soon as the door was shut, I locked it.

I hit the gas. Tears streamed down my cheeks as I drove away, forcing my burning eyes to stay on the road. I could hardly breathe, hardly think. I couldn't leave my mate. *Turn around. Fight.*

There was a terrible pained sound filling the car, and it took me a minute to realize it was me.

CHAPTER TWENTY

JETT

*S*hards of glass clung to my fur as I rose back up to my paws. It was four against one, but all I could think about was the broken window, and how it belonged to my daughter's bedroom.

If the Greenville City Pack had any honor, they'd leave my family out of this. But if they had any honor, they wouldn't have come to my house in the middle of the night, stalking us in the darkness.

The second largest among the wolves was the one I recognized, the one who'd stabbed me in the neck and thrown me in his trunk. The one who'd tried to kill me in that field—Tiny.

The others were strangers, and just as dangerous. The largest hung back, while Tiny and his friends slowly closed in on me, taking turns tearing into my flesh.

"Where is he?" The largest growled in the shifter tongue. He had to be Briggs, the one who'd organized everything, including the betrayal of the roving chapter.

I knew Brick's mistake would cost us, that it would embolden Greenville. I just hadn't thought it wouldn't bring them here. We should have left town, gone to Paige's apartment. But it was too late for that now.

"There's no one here for you," I growled.

"This is him, boss." Tiny said in the shifter tongue.

Fucker. How had they known where to find me?

The card...I'd handed him my business card back in Greenville. They had my name. That's how they'd found us.

I'd fucked up so bad.

Without waiting for a reply, Tiny dove at me again. This strike, I dodged in time. I just had to keep them away from the house. I had to keep them outside long enough for—

Engines roared on approach, the distinct sound of motorcycles that meant my brothers had arrived. I hadn't noticed until they were close. But now, this was over.

"Run while you can," I growled.

"We won't leave without Lars." Briggs held his head high.

Proud bastard should have considered what war meant before starting one.

"He's been released." Hawke rounded the building in human form, flanked by a big ass grizzly, Brick, and a wolf, Ray.

"Where?" Briggs growled.

"Edge of town." Hawke slid his hands into his pockets, completely at ease, completely in control of the situation. I didn't know how he did it, but when it came down to it, Hawke always looked like he had his shit together. Just like Brick always looked like he was going to rip someone's throat out. He would, in a heartbeat, and he'd enjoy it.

"Now that we've finally got your attention, tell me why." Hawke narrowed his eyes at Briggs.

"Why what? I don't even know you people." Briggs shook his muzzle, hot steam billowing from his nostrils.

"Why your second—"

Tiny bounded toward Hawke. Brick moved in front of

the alpha, but not before I dove at the bastard. If anyone was getting a piece of this asshole, it was me.

"No!" Briggs commanded his second, but Tiny wasn't listening. He was the one who'd started all of this. I'd end it.

I caught his leg in my jaw and threw my weight into his side. Tiny barreled over, falling to the ground.

"Stop," Briggs barked, but he wasn't my alpha. I stalked forward, standing over the bastard who had drugged me, thrown me in a trunk, and beaten me nearly to death. Worse, he had come to my home...to my family.

"Don't fucking move," I growled to Tiny, who lay still at my paws. This ended tonight, one way or another. But I wasn't rabid like him; I'd wait for Hawke to give the word.

"Tell me why you betrayed the Silent Butchers," Hawke said.

"You're...Silent Butchers..." Briggs shifted back to human form.

Briggs was leaving himself vulnerable by shifting, naked.

Hawke just looked at him. "Why would you be here if you didn't know that?"

"You took our man." Briggs crossed his arms.

"Only after you tried to kill ours."

Briggs blinked hard and shook his head. "I did no such thing."

I couldn't sense a lie in his words. Why couldn't I hear it?

"Tell me you're not Briggs." Hawke stared the other alpha down.

"I am." Briggs took a step closer, holding a hand out to tell his backup to stay put.

Naked and alone, Briggs handed Hawke a clear advantage...*but why?* That advantage doubled as he walked away from his men.

"I'm Hunter Briggs, alpha of the Greenville City Pack.

The only interaction I've had with your MC is when my uncle hired some of your guys to slaughter my family."

What the fuck?

"He turned on them, as he turned on his own kin, but none of that was my doing." Briggs stopped two feet from Brick. One false move and the grizzly would tear him apart.

But Briggs's words rang true, and I thought back to what Draper had told me. He'd said Briggs, but not which Briggs. Why the hell would we assume there were a bunch of them?

"I believe you." Hawke crossed his arms. "But that doesn't absolve you of the assault of my second."

Briggs cocked his head to the side. "What are you talking about?"

"Your man, Tiny, tried to kill my guy when he came to you for a peaceful meeting."

"I never heard a word of this, not the meeting or any attack."

Briggs again spoke the truth.

All eyes turned to Tiny on the ground.

"It's my job. I was protecting you," Tiny said in the shifter tongue. There was no lie in his words either. He *believed* he was doing the right thing.

Fucking idiot.

Briggs's jaw tightened before he turned back to Hawke. "You took one of mine after one of mine assaulted one of yours. Upon the safe return of Lars, I wish no further quarrel with you. Peace?" Briggs offered his hand.

Hawke looked to me. He didn't need my approval, but I appreciated the gesture, and nodded.

"Deal with your wild dog," Hawke said.

Briggs spared a glance at Brick, who was seething a bit, but otherwise still.

"I will."

"And your uncle, the one responsible for the deaths and capture of the roving chapter?" Hawke asked.

"Phillip Briggs—exiled," Briggs replied.

"And if the Butchers find him?"

Briggs sucked in a deep breath. "He's dug his own grave. When the consequences of his actions catch up with him, he deserves his fate. I'm actually surprised you haven't found him yet. My father informed the Butchers of his location."

Again, I recalled what Draper had said. He'd told me that when they hunted down Briggs, that was when the Tribunal had apprehended the roving pack. It seemed this Phillip Briggs might still be on the run. If so, maybe one of the other chapters would want to hunt him down. Maybe Brick would. Either way, I was out.

Hawke considered Briggs, nodded, and accepted his hand.

The two shook, and just like that, there was peace. I looked down at Tiny and took a step back. He rose to his paws and shifted back to human form.

The other Greenville wolf did the same.

Content that it was over, I shifted back, too, leaving Brick as the only beast among us.

The look Briggs shot Tiny told me he'd keep his word.

It was really over.

I had to tell Paige the good news.

But Hawke grabbed my arm as I went to pass. "I'm taking your advice."

"What advice?"

"I'm dissolving the MC in Ashwood."

Brick growled, a deep roar coming from such a big ass bear.

Hawke looked to Brick. "Anyone who wants to join another chapter would be welcome to do so."

Brick wouldn't leave. Ray would, given his dream was to join the Butchers. But I had a hard time imagining Brick going anywhere Shaundra wasn't. I'd seen the way he looked at her. It was the same way I looked at Paige.

I nodded to Hawke. "I need to check on my family."

"Sure."

I ran past the others to the front of the house, and found the door already open. Bile rose in my throat as I raced inside to my daughter's room, and found it empty. "Paige? Evelyn?"

I ran back to the doorway and watched the line of bikes leaving the driveway. But Paige's car...my family was already gone.

CHAPTER TWENTY-ONE

PAIGE

"I want to go home." Evie curled her little body around the stuffed rhino Jett had given her, a ball on the couch hiding beneath a throw blanket. I'd tried to get her to settle into my bed, but she'd refused.

"I want to go home, too." Except I was home, back in my apartment. I sat down beside Evie and rubbed her back. Neither of us had slept, and now the sun was already up. I wanted to pace. I wanted to scream. I wanted to cry. None of that would change what had happened.

I checked my phone for the thousandth time, praying that he'd called or sent a text and I'd just missed it. I had to know that Jett was okay. I'd left him three messages already, and he'd call when he could, wouldn't he?

He would. He could. He was fine. Everything was going to be fine.

I closed my eyes and fought for composure when all I wanted to do was break down.

"I want my daddy."

"I know." I lay beside Evie and held her. I checked my phone again. Nothing.

"Can we go back?"

I pet her hair softly and her eyes slid shut.

"...I want...I want...to go home." Her chest rose and fell as she drifted off to sleep.

Tears streamed down my cheeks. I couldn't stop it once it started, but I wasn't sure I wanted to. There was something cathartic about letting go, just a little, when I knew she couldn't see me. I held my mouth shut hard, so as not to make a sound, and I let myself cry.

We'd come here because I didn't know where else to go. But this apartment, it wasn't my home anymore. Jett was my home. We couldn't live a life where wolves showed up in the night to harm us. But I couldn't live without him, either. We were mates. That was supposed to be it, the key to our happily ever after. We were supposed to have a bunch of kids, and steal kisses in the quiet moments when the chaos finally stilled. We were supposed to share picnics in the woods and learn every story the other person had to tell. Being mates meant love and contentment and finishing each other's sentences. Not tears and fear...not *this*.

I closed my eyes and tried to rest. My body hurt, my heart was shattered. I was a broken mess, and I needed to sleep. Unwanted images flashed through my head—of our home burning, of my mate bloodied. His bright blue eyes faded as he lay on the ground, unmoving.

I shook the thought, and the idea of sleep, and headed to the kitchen for some coffee. There wasn't a whole lot in the fridge. My veggies would need to be tossed, but the coffee— that was still good.

A gentle knocking came from the door. It was probably just Mrs. Foster from next door checking in since my car was parked out front and she'd know I was back. She was sweet, and I could use any distraction right about now. Maybe the stray cat, Graybeard, had snuck inside the building again. I bet Evie would love him.

I opened the door and *he* was there—blue eyes tired, brown hair a wild mess. Not my favorite cat, but even better, my mate. He leaned on the doorframe like he couldn't quite stand on his own, and the scent of blood overwhelmed everything else. It overwhelmed everything but my need to touch him.

I threw my arms around him, only realizing after he cringed that I was hurting him.

"Are you...I can't believe...what the hell happened?" My words came out a tumbled rush, my heart full and my head swimming.

"It's over. Are you two okay? Where's Evelyn?"

"We're fine. She's on the couch." *Everything's fine.*

Jett crept over and peeked at her. The admiration in his eyes when he watched her sleep filled me with joy. Jett was here. There wasn't just sadness or a touch of happiness—I was exhausted with relief.

We went back to the kitchen, far enough away not to disturb Evie.

"Nice apartment," he said.

I snorted. The apartment was fine, but that's not what we needed to talk about.

"How do you know this won't happen again?" I stared into his deep blue eyes, searching for answers.

"There's peace between the packs," he said.

"What about the MC?"

"The Ashwood chapter's disbanded. Butcher trouble isn't our problem anymore."

I couldn't believe it. It was too good to be true. "Disbanded? And everyone's okay with that?"

Jett shrugged. "They will be, or they'll join a different

chapter. But they're not what matters. All that matters to me are you and—"

"Daddy!" Evie hopped off the couch and threw herself around Jett's legs.

"All that matters is that I have you two. My girls. My family."

EPILOGUE

PAIGE

I used to believe in love at first sight.

I used to believe in soulmates, that there was one perfect person out in the world that complemented you in every way. Love takes work.

There is no one magic moment where everything wondrously becomes easy for the rest of eternity. Love is a commitment, a promise to ride out the bad times, knowing that with work and time, the good is worth fighting for.

Forever doesn't just happen. It's a choice, one worth compromising for. It's finding that person who will compromise for you, too.

It's the little moments holding hands or watching movies snuggled up on the sofa. It's deciding to share the last cookie instead of eating it yourself. It's stepping up when it's easier to walk away, because love endures.

It's not waiting for an unrealistically flawless person to fall into your life, but fighting for someone who's worth fighting for. It's always being there and never giving up.

Love isn't always easy, but the best things in life never are.

*T*hat was it. I finally finished my article. I titled it *Forget Mr. Right. Snag Mr. Worthwhile.* A quick tap on *send,* and I shut my laptop.

A weight lifted and I bounced with every step. With everything else we'd been through, articulating my thoughts on relationships was easy-peasy. Plenty of time left to prep for the picnic.

Graybeard weaved between my legs, purring. I'd been sad leaving him behind in the city, thinking he was a wild man and needed his space, but somehow, he'd followed us here. I still hadn't figured out if he'd found his own way, or if Jett had gone back for him. My guess was the second.

The doorbell rang, and I popped a cherry tomato from one of the platters in my mouth as I walked past the brand spanking new stainless appliances and butcher block countertops. The remodel had gone more quickly than I'd expected, and I was in love with the results.

A splash of tart acidity met my tongue as I crushed the orb between my teeth. At the door, I'd expected it to be Shaundra, or even Hawke. But it wasn't.

It was Linda.

"Hey." I squeezed her in a quick hug before realizing it might not be the best thing. "Sorry. Was that too rough? How's your hip?"

She laughed. "I'm okay. It was nice. How are you?"

"I'm good. This is a nice surprise."

We'd picked up all of Evie's things, and she'd been out to visit twice. I had said to come by anytime, but I hadn't thought she would.

"I was going through some old boxes and I found one with Marla's old toys. I thought Evelyn might like to have them."

"That's so sweet. I'm sure she'll love it. Do you want to come in and—"

"Grandma!" Evie left Jett and Lacey in the dust as she ran up and greeted her grandmother just like I had, with unrestrained enthusiasm.

"It's so good to see you." Linda patted her back. "I think you grow an inch or five every time I see you."

"What? No way. Want to play with me and Lacey?"

Now it was Linda's and Evie's turn to do the same thing—look at me with big puppy dog eyes.

"Of course you can," I said.

Evie grabbed her grandmother in one hand and her friend in the other and pulled them back the hall.

"Don't make her sit on the floor to play," I called after them.

Jett crowded me in the best way, and I took him in—perfectly fitted suit, fresh spiced scent, and the perfect five o'clock shadow. He'd been working at a law firm that had flexible hours and allowed him to be home in time to pick up Evie from the bus every day. And he still helped the pack with paperwork for their security company. I didn't know how he did so much, but he managed it.

I loved him in a suit as much as I loved him in his leather jacket and jeans. I liked stripping him out of his clothes best of all.

His lips curved up and his eyes darkened as he looked me over. "Something smells good."

"Oh, just a few dishes I threw together for the picnic."

"I meant you."

He nipped my chin and captured my lips. I would never grow tired of kissing this man, of being held by him, being loved by him.

The rumble of engines approached from outside, while squeals of delight carried through the cabin. It was time for a pack picnic, so our fun would have to wait. I didn't mind. We had all the time in the world, because we were mates. And we were forever.

ABOUT THE AUTHOR

Keyboard ninja, late-blooming bibliophile, proud geek, animal lover, eternal optimist, visual artist.

Keira Blackwood writes steamy paranormal romance full of suspense, action, and a dash of humor. No cheating. Always a happily-ever-after ending.

www.keirablackwood.com

Printed in Great Britain
by Amazon

23937602R00108